BUTTERCUP COTTAGE AND SLOBBER DOM, DOM

This illustrated children's story revolves around the Chadwick family, who are driven far away from their home by a spiteful sprite, Slobber Dom, Dom, and his cat, Jingle Black Jack. As they endeavour to find their way home, the Chadwicks encounter many strange and wonderful creatures, including a troll, a leprechaun and a kingdom of fairies, who help them on their journey. However, the evil antics of Slobber Dom, Dom, his cat and a wicked witch haunt and impede the intrepid family's attempt to return to Buttercup Cottage.

BUTTERCUP COTTAGE AND SLOBBER DOM, DOM
A children's Story

Harrison Faibien Byron

ARTHUR H. STOCKWELL LTD.
Torrs Park   Ilfracombe   Devon
Established 1898
www.ahstockwell.co.uk

British Library Cataloguing-in-Publication Data.
A catalogue record for this book is available
from the British Library.

ISBN 0-7223-3782-5
ISBN 978-0-7223-3782-0
Printed in Great Britain by
Arthur H. Stockwell Ltd.
Torrs Park   Ilfracombe
Devon

About the Author

Having been born at the cottage hospital in Lutterworth, Leicestershire in 1954, I attended Lutterworth High School and Lutterworth Grammar School, where I excelled in art.

I have been an established, prolific poet for the last twelve years, writing classical poetry, love poems and works of prose, and have a personal collection of over 800 poems, 700 love songs, 500 coloured illustrations and numerous inventions filed away. I have submitted work to *Poetry Now* and the International Society of Poetry in America on a regular basis. Also I have been writing children's short stories with a collection of eighteen published alongside other authors.

My interests are listening to classical music, collecting antiques, oil-painting and reading all the great poets of yesteryear, especially those of the early nineteenth century, such as Lord Byron, Keats, Shelley and Mary Shelley.

Having been in the Royal Navy for eight years (1971–1978), I had the good fortune to be selected to serve aboard HMS *Victory* in Portsmouth Dockyard as a guide for a two-year stay where I indulged myself in reading Napoleonic history and the glory of Nelson's victories. I have always been an avid book-lover, especially history of a bygone age.

I also indulge in drawing and painting, especially portraiture works, when the mood takes me. I have three oil paintings, and various other coloured pencil works which are framed.

After being in the Royal Navy I served in the merchant navy for five years, serving aboard a large oil tanker for a six-month stay in the Persian Gulf regions, and afterwards I joined the merchant supply fleets, working mainly in the North Sea, being based at Montrose and Aberdeen, supplying all the oil rigs in dangerous conditions. Afterwards I was employed on supply boats out in West Africa, visiting Gabon, Cameroon and Nigeria, where death is commonplace amongst its French-speaking peoples.

Whilst in the Royal Navy I served aboard HMS *Tiger*, a large battle cruiser, which was refitted and carried three Sea King helicopters, with a crew of 850 men and officers aboard. We visited many exciting places, including Gibraltar, Malta, Italy, Singapore, Hong Kong, Malaysia, the Persian Gulf states, Mombasa and many more Mediterranean destinations where I gained a lot of experience. From there I served aboard HMS *Hydra*, a survey vessel, for eighteen months' duration, visiting the Seychelles in the Indian Ocean for three months, and other destinations, such as the United Arab Emirates and Iran.

Contents

Chapter One

Buttercup Cottage

Once upon a time, long, long ago in the eighteenth century, there lived three little boys and three little girls. They lived deep in the forest with their frail grandmother and grandfather, who were named Arthur and Bella Chadwick, in a large thatched house named Buttercup Cottage. Around the beautiful cottage grew wild ivy creepers and a rose bush with thorns.

The three boys' names were Joe, Billy and Peter, aged seven, eight and nine. The three girls were Samantha, Suzanne and Alberta, aged six, ten and twelve.

They had all lived in the forest for over three years after moving away from the city, where folk lived in turmoil, so as to live a more simple, peaceful life, away from all the smoke and other pollution that cities across the world make.

But this wasn't a tranquil forest – far from it. For in reality it was an enchanted wood where magical and devious things would happen.

At night, after playing games of hide-and-seek and hopscotch, their grandfather would read them a fairy story full of wonder and enchantment. Then they would place under their pillows a wish list containing all the things they wanted to come true. Once they were all tucked up safely in their warm beds they were soon in the Land of Nod, all snoring loudly and dreaming of the things they had wished for.

Now, in the forest of Blackbird Wood there were many mischievous, magical sprites, gnomes, fairy people, salamanders and invisible deities who just could not stop themselves having a bit of sport and fun. One particular sprite, named Slobber Dom, Dom, loved to play tricks and pranks upon any persons unlucky enough to travel deeply into the forest to his territory – they would regret their foolish actions for the remainder of their lives.

When the midnight hour came, things began to happen inside and outside the cottage where the Chadwicks slept like rabbits in their hutches.

While out on his nightly patrol, the devilish sprite came flying through the dark skies and, by sheer chance, stumbled across Buttercup Cottage. He flew around the entire garden and house. The sprite laughed and smiled to himself so much that he nearly fell into the pigsty. The pigs became annoyed and frightened him away from the pen.

'Oh,' thought the sprite, 'I'll teach them a thing or two.' He put a spell on them, and half became stone pigs, who could not fumble and grumble any more, and the other half were changed into pink piglets who now had wings like dragonflies. They flew off into the night air, squeaking and making other noises that pigs make.

He then put a magical black cat, named Jingle Black Jack, in amongst the pigeons. They all fluttered their wings and the night sky was filled with the dust of their feathers falling down to the ground.

"Oh, what a clever sprite I am!" spoke the sprite to himself. "Now I need another bright plan." He chuckled all the more, and sat amongst some logs, which gave way and he fell head over heels into some cow sludge, making his clothes all dirty and ruffled.

The moonbeam smiled with rays of light over the whole of the cottage, as the sprite thought up another bright prank. He reached right down inside his green

10

pantaloons and fetched out a green velvet bag. He took some magical powder from this pouch and sprinkled it all around the confines of the cottage in Blackbird Wood. After carefully sprinkling this magic powder over the roots of the wild ivy and rose thorns, puff went a cloud of fine white smoke, and there to his astonishment grew wild plants, growing bigger and bigger, climbing all over the place during his bewitching hour of mischief.

Now, taking off in flight, the sprite with his dastardly actions flew carefully, but not too closely, just out of reach of the creepers and thorns. He could hear sounds coming from within the cottage.

The children woke first to the sounds and noise of thunder cracking.

"Oh, what on earth could the matter be? Is it a trick of my imagination? Oh, what could be wrong?" thought Billy and Alberta.

To their horror, the house was so dimly lit that they lit their candles and went on an investigation. They shook the other frightened children from their beds.

The glass in the windows began to break and explode, because now it was the hour of midnight, and the creepers and rose thorns had climbed so fast they were strangling all of the cottage with their terrible power. Before daylight had arrived, the shoots and stems had climbed all over the thatched roof and penetrated any cracks and holes.

The children ran from room to room, shouting and screaming from the tops of their lungs.

Samantha and Joe found their grandparents smothered and entombed by the creepers, rose thorns and other vegetation, which now overlapped the frightened couple in their own beds. For now they were both trapped.

'What on earth do we do now?' thought Samantha.

With trepidation and a little daring, she spoke out aloud. "Oh, Grandmother, what has happened to you and Papa?"

The Ivy and Rose Thorns Covered
the Whole of the Cottage.

They answered bravely, "We do not know, my child. At least we can speak to you, but we cannot move our legs or torsos."

"You'll have to get a saw from outside," said Papa.

"But we can't," said Joe.

"But why?" said Papa.

"Because all the ivy and rose thorns have taken root over the whole of the cottage from earth to sky."

The two children went back to the kitchen to see if there were any suitable tools to free their grandparents from their dilemma.

Joe grabbed a kitchen knife and tried and tried with all of his strength to cut through the thick stems of the ivy – but to no avail, they were too tough. The only place the creepers had not gone was down the chimney pot.

Slobber Dom, Dom, the bad mischievous sprite, thought to himself, 'What have I done? What a mess I have caused! How do I undo the wicked spell? Mother Fairy will be cross when she finds out what I have done!'

An idea crossed his mind. He flew like a dark orb down and down into the bottom of the chimney stack and stood on the grate like a king, with his green pants, red jacket and a crown upon his head.

The children noticed him, with startled looks upon their faces.

"Who are you?" said Billy. "Are you real? Are you a garden gnome that's come to steal?"

"You do smell a great deal," said Alberta, the oldest of the children.

Now, Slobber Dom, Dom was not amused with their childish remarks and observations. He spoke accordingly: "Me? Smell? How can that be, for I am the leader of the fairies in Blackbird Wood? Can you not see my crown of golden jewels? The greatest fairy that ever lived has come to save you. And if you don't follow my rules, I'll turn you all into rabbits and hares, or I might change you into donkeys and goats. That would be a fine thing, don't you think?"

"You don't sound very nice, as a good fairy should. And you do smell like a cow in her field grazing," laughed Peter.

This made the sprite rather mad. He waved his arms and chanted, "Wacksie, packsie, daskie."

Puff went Peter, who turned into a beautiful butterfly which flew around the room.

The children became frightened and intrigued.

"What have you done, bad sprite? Change him back immediately," cried out Billy.

"Oh, but I cannot, because I don't have my spell book with me. I have left it back at camp in the fairy kingdom of Annatasia."

"But you must find it! Quickly now, fly away back to where you have come from," pleaded Samantha.

"Oh, but it is miles away – over twenty-five miles, I should reckon. And, besides, Mother Fairy will be mad as a wild donkey when she finds out what I have done."

Arthur Chadwick shouted for help from his bedroom. He could hardly breathe because the vines had become stronger, and Bella Chadwick had fallen into a deep sleep.

The bad sprite relented and said he would try his hardest to untangle their grandparents from the horrible creeping vines. For ten minutes he tried to remember the special magical spells which would free them. He said all manner of silly words until, at last, he got it right, and with the words "Rosebuds and thorns, unwrap your deadly horns" the creepers lost their grip, and withered away from them. "How's that, my friendly cottage chums? I have saved them at last."

"Oh, you are a clever sprite – but also a naughty one. If it wasn't for you, we would not be in this mess that you have caused," said Alberta excitedly.

Bella Chadwick awoke and brushed away from her face all the dusty leaves that had so cruelly surrounded her. She and Papa fled their tiny room in a fine twitter and ran to the safety of the dining area, where, to their amazement, stood the cheeky bad sprite.

Now, at his side was his magical cat, Jingle Black Jack, who had terrorised the animals into a mad frenzy in and around the animal pens. He looked quite menacing, with the pupils in his black and yellow eyes enlarged. Jingle Black Jack sat beside his master, pawing with his outstretched claws and with an evil grin upon his wicked mouth. "Oh, what shall we do now, Slobber Dom, Dom? Eat them all alive in one sitting? I'm rather hungry after my chase around the cottage. It would be nice to set my knife and fork upon the large kitchen table, with a nice napkin under my chin, don't you think, children from Buttercup Cottage?"

The sprite stamped on the cat's long black tail, and he squealed and screeched mighty loudly. The sprite declared, "Bide your tongue, Jingle Black Jack, if you know what's good for you. You'll frighten everyone to death."

The cat frowned with an undisciplined deceiving mind, and snarled at everyone in the room. Jingle Black Jack was cunning, right enough – not like your normal domesticated cat would be. He was not a cat that you would take home to meet Mother. He wasn't friendly at all.

Arthur Chadwick spoke out: "What is this all about? Why have you come here? What have you done to my sweet cottage in Blackbird Wood? We are friendly people. It will cost you dearly for all the damage you and that rascal of a cat have done to my property!"

"Well said, Granddad," replied Alberta. "It's about time they had a good telling-off. Who do they both think they are?" she exclaimed.

"Who are we?" shouted the dastardly sprite, his temper now boiling over again. "We are the kings of the forest and wood, me and my old buddy, Jingle Black Jack. If you don't do as you're told, we'll set fire to all that you own. Then see how you like it! What about that, then?" he said cheerfully.

Joe Caught Peter.

"Oh no you won't," said Samantha. "I'll report you to the head fairy, however long it takes, and then you'll get what's coming to you both. Then we will see what happens, won't we?"

Then, all of a sudden, the bad sprite and the cat vanished from sight, both flying up through the chimney pot.

They were all startled by what had taken place in their beautiful cottage. There seemed no way out. The door entrance was just a mass of vines and leaves, and every other entrance was also blocked.

The youngest boy, Joe, caught Peter, now a wandering butterfly, in his hands and asked for a container to put him in so he could not escape and fly away.

Soon Suzanne came to the rescue. She found a glass bottle and placed him inside carefully, so as not to damage him in any way. The neck of the bottle was slim, and he would not be able to find his way out because of his delicate wings.

What bad and dangerous sprites they were! Was it a bad dream they were all experiencing? It was so surreal and unbelievable. What magic had they used? It was surely a game of the sprites with bad mischief as the main culprit. Were there witches on broomsticks that travelled the forest unnoticed? Or were there darker forces at work – deadly ghosts and bad angels? It was anybody's guess.

The whole family checked everywhere for a suitable escape or a solution to this most troubling nightmare.

Alberta tried to soothe the youngest child, Samantha, who was frightfully nervous. She had started to cry, and large tears were now streaming down her rosy cheeks. She was fretting badly that the awful sprite would come back and eat them all up for his dinner.

Then, with great excitement and anticipation, Billy came skidding across the floor to where the other children were huddled, discussing events. He yelled that he had seen an orb of light chasing him from the kitchen area. He tripped over the old carpet rug and landed smack upon his bottom. He had displaced the heavy rug from its position near the hearth, and, to everyone's astonishment, there was what looked like an old trapdoor in the floor. Unexpectedly a miracle had occurred in the nick of time.

What heavenly saviour was this? Or was it the sprite again, with some dubious plan up his sleeve? Or was it purely coincidence, a trick of fortune at the last hour?

Now, with delight and surprise in his eyes, Billy pulled upon the trapdoor's iron ring, but it did not open. Then, with an iron lever that Samantha fetched from the kitchen, he managed to open the hatch in the floor and a waft of air blew upwards from the dark recess in front of their eyes.

Granddad Chadwick fetched an old miner's oil lamp, which he lit with a striker, and peered down, in front of everyone else, to see more clearly what may be down there. He exclaimed, "There is a stone stairway going down for about fifteen feet, but there are too many cobwebs to see properly. I need more light."

"Do you think it's wise, Granddad, to go down into that black hole?" enquired Suzanne.

"It might be a trap, set by the bad sprite to lure us in," shouted out Billy.

"I bet there's a million giant cobwebs down there, where giant spiders eat their prey, and human bones are piled sky-high – not a place I would like to go," butted in Alberta.

"But we have no alternative," said Grandma Chadwick alarmingly. "The vines are everywhere – look, they are everywhere. We only have this chance left to escape," she declared, whilst looking at everyone with a reassuring heart. "If we don't, we surely will die! We only have a week's supply of food left, and the water pump is outside. That only gives us three days, if we're lucky."

"Who's prepared to search the tunnel? As you know,

children, Grandma and I are frail, and are not as quick as we would like to be."

Billy spoke up: "I will go down and inspect this dark world. I'm not frightened of any sprite, or dragon, or demon of the underworld, because I am brave, like a knight in shining armour – one who sits at King Arthur's Round Table."

And, at his brave words, everyone clapped enthusiastically. The girls hugged him, and gave him their support in daring the unknown worlds of the universe.

"I will take with me a rope, a knife and some water, just in case I get lost. I shall not go too far first time, but I will be cunning and safe like a vulpine – a fox who protects her lair and cubs. If I am not back in half an hour, then I am finished, and I would not like any of you to follow me, but say grace and prayers to Him that made the world and its great creatures."

"Oh, Billy, are you sure of your intentions?" whispered Suzanne.

"Yes, my dear sister. We have got to try to find a way to change our eldest brother back into a human being. It's not fair that he should stay a butterfly for ever, especially now he is trapped in a bottle, with no friends or nectar to drink."

Soon, Billy was ready to begin his frightful challenge, and proceed with good faith down into the murky depths. They all helped to dress him accordingly with all the necessary equipment that he would carry with him.

Chapter Two

The Dark Tunnel

With a coil of rope around his head and chest, Billy went down, carrying the old oil lamp with him. He stopped on the bottom step and peered all about him. While knocking the dusty cobwebs away from his face, neck and shoulders, he shone his lamp all around. He could hear water dripping in the distance, and walked ahead, groping his way along the walls, which were green and slimy.

He heard his family's voices melting away in the distance: "Are you all right, Billy?" "What's down there?" "Please take care of yourself."

He shouted back, his voice echoing: "I'm okay. There's nothing to worry about."

After going about fifty feet, the dark recess got bigger and bigger, and now he was in what looked like a large cavern, with about twenty-five different tunnels all leading their separate ways off into the unknown, around the whole circumference of the cave.

'What on earth is this?' thought Billy to himself while pondering his next action.

Which tunnel would he venture along first? There were so many to choose from. He was almost spoilt for choice.

'Will it really matter which one?' he thought.

There seemed to be tiny shafts of light further down

each tunnel, allowing the eye to see better, with some clarity and vision. He was glad of that, for the oil lamp would not last for ever. It reassured him greatly and gave him added confidence to explore further.

Cunning as he was, Billy picked up a large rock and placed it by the entrance to one of the many tunnels, so when he came back, if at all, he would know that he had been in that one.

So off he blindly went, searching, feeling a little frightened. He could feel his nerves stretching inside his stomach. Would he go on, or turn and run away? Flight seemed a good alternative. It was easy to be bold and brash with courageous words, but it was action, not words that counted the most. He had to make up his mind one way or the other.

'If only I was an adult, a man, not a mere child of eight years. Why? Oh, why me?' he thought placidly.

Then, by chance, some way off in the tunnel he could see activity going on, like a flash before his eyes. Was he seeing things in their true reality? There, to his amazement, was an army of what looked like large worker ants, all fetching and carrying food for their silken grubs. This frightened Billy at first, and he stayed in the shadows while working out if they were friendly.

Surely he would be detected, and consumed as an enemy of the colony? If he ran backwards, they would chase him, and take him back to their lair and their queen.

Suddenly an ant came along that was different from the rest. He seemed to be golden in colour, like a shining glow, pure as gold can be. Never had Billy seen any gold before, but intuitively he knew what it was.

He presumed it to be the leader ant.

The ant raised himself up onto his hind legs and spoke excitedly to Billy: "Oh, my dear, dear, dear, and what are you doing down here, may I ask? My name's Christopher, King of the Ants, king of all the underworld and passageways. When we become king or queen, we automatically turn into pure gold. So what can I do for you, young fellow?" he asked.

"Are you going to hurt me, or even eat me up?" cried out Billy.

"Oh, you are big and fat, and I think you would make quite a nice dinner for all our hungry worker ants. Oh, do excuse me, young man, I'm only having you on – a bad joke, one might say. And what is your name, young boy? Are you lost? Can I be of assistance?"

"If what you say you are is true, then I shall bow before you, Majesty, King of the Ants, like this, with the sweep of my right arm, and acknowledge you as such a mighty ant. My name is Billy Chadwick, and I have been forced down here to search for a place to escape from the evils of the forest and woods above. Back yonder, through this maze of tunnels, my whole family is trapped inside Buttercup Cottage by terrible rose thorns and wild ivy creepers, which have grown and grown all over the house, and there is no possible way out. A bad sprite is responsible. It is he who has put a wicked black spell upon the place. Also, my eldest brother, Peter, has been turned into a flying insect, a butterfly, and is now kept in a glass bottle for his own good. Oh, you must help me if you can, King Christopher of the underworld."

"Oh, Billy Chadwick, you are in a poor way, aren't you? Let me think a while. Ha, yes, I have the perfect solution. You and your family can come to me and my large family of worker ants, and we will look after you and feed you. We are born from sweet nectar and honey, straight from the pot, one might say. Over there, Billy Chadwick, look at all the young ants flying from their cocoons and nests, straight from birth. But do tell me more, Billy Chadwick; who is this wicked sprite you mention? I do hope it's not the creature that I am thinking of. It wouldn't be Slobber Dom, Dom, would it?"

"How did you guess that? Are you using magic of sorts?" said Billy excitedly.

"Magic? No, there's no magic to it. We do everything

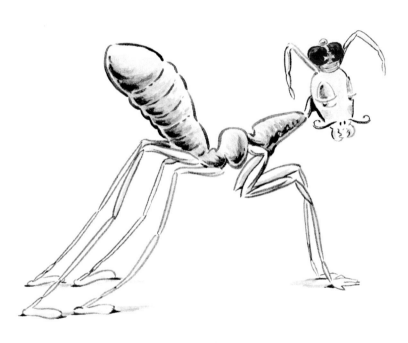

Christopher, King of the Ants.

from the book, as nature expects us to. We work hard all day, and sleep by night, gathering up all of our precious honey. We are wise ants – after all, I have my gracious queen to look after. She's a beautiful sweet queen who treats us with great admiration and respect – especially me, as I am her king and friend. And while we're on the subject of magic, what else has the sprite done?"

"Oh, he has a wicked black cat named Jingle Black Jack, who has frightened all of our livestock away, and they have threatened to eat us for supper, amongst other horrible things they would like to do," explained Billy.

"I thought as much. Both of them have been reported and reported and reported, but we never seem to be able to catch them. Mother Fairy knows only too well of their irresponsible nature, and they are on her most-wanted list of naughty, mischievous persons. He and his cat have a bad, bad attitude. They think it's quite funny to watch their unfortunate victims squeal and squirm in a most frightening manner. All we can do is report back about their unruly behaviour in Blackbird Wood."

"Do you think you'll ever catch them?" exclaimed Billy, always wanting to know more.

"Oh, my lost friend, they are naughty sprites who are undeveloped. They live on a lower plane and frequency – unripe, as one might say. So there you have it, young man – not a very nice situation to be in." The king ant now smiled at Billy Chadwick, and told him to go back quickly and fetch the rest of his bewildered family, whilst he got the worker ants to build another golden passageway before the day's end.

So Billy set off again and headed the way he had come. He had been gone for twenty minutes already. When Billy returned to the main entrance he heard a croaking sound coming from one of the other tunnels. Without further ado, he shone in his oil lamp to see what on earth the matter was, and behold! there was a large green slimy frog or toad some thirty or so feet in the distance.

Hoping the frog could speak, Billy now bravely challenged the giant creature: "Are you the genuine thing, Mr Frog? Do excuse me – my name's Billy Chadwick."

The frog was pleased as Punch, and outstretched his belly into a large balloon shape, which startled Billy Chadwick so much that he tried to flee the tunnel quickly, but the frog jumped five feet at a time, straight to Billy's side.

"Oh yes, I am really a frog. They call me Flipper Green Roger. I was once a froglet, and these past months or days, I can't remember which, I've been down here on my own just wandering and wandering about with no way out. I was sent down here by the wicked witch named Silba. She uses me for casting wicked spells, which I've got rather fed up with just lately. When the full moon is out, she throws sugar and cream, cod liver oil and jam, fruits and juices, pepper and salt, apple sauce with vinegar, grease and soap, and all manner of things into a large black cauldron, which is situated in her enormous cave in the woods above this network of tunnels, and mixes them together. She then smears the concoction all over my beautiful smooth skin. And when I try to escape from the underworld, she uses special tricks and builds walls at either end inside the tunnel, preventing me from ever getting out, which is a very cruel thing for a wandering frog like me to experience."

"Oh, don't worry, Flipper Green Roger, you can tag along with me. I'm on the way to fetch the rest of my family, and I'll show you the way out if we're lucky enough."

"Oh, you're so kind, Sir Billy Chadwick, and I am very grateful for your kindness," said Mr Frog.

So off they went back to the cellar steps of Buttercup Cottage and Billy shouted up the stone stairway with enthusiasm and pride, "Granddad, are you there? Come quickly with all the family. I've met some great friends down here, and they may be able to help us. Hello! Is anyone there?"

"Yes, Billy, my brave grandchild. We'll pack our things quickly and come down the steps to meet you."

And so they did, one by one. Each family member braved the dark cellar with much bravado and expectation in their hearts.

"Exploration isn't one of my best attributes," shouted out Bella Chadwick. "I do hope we're all going to be safe down here, Billy."

"Oh, yes, Grandma, I can vouch for it. From what I have seen, there's no real danger as yet."

When they had all mustered down in the tunnel, everyone, except for Billy, became hysterical at being confronted with the giant frog.

"Oh, Billy, what is this monster doing down here? Are my eyes seeing what I think they are seeing?" exclaimed Albert and Arthur.

"Oh, do not worry or fret, this is Flipper Green Roger, the most friendly and sincere frog that you're ever likely to meet. He's lost as we are. So do calm down everyone and do as I say," shouted Billy excitedly. "And he can talk the Queen's English, can't you, Flipper?"

"Oh, yes, my faithful master, I can hop at least forty feet, and I can duck and dive from side to side, and I can hide without being noticed, because my skin changes to many different colours."

"Oh, you are a smart frog, Flipper," said Samantha.

"So what do we do now, Billy?" everyone shouted at once.

"Oh, follow me and Flipper, and we will show you some amazing things down here."

Billy hoped that the rock he placed at the end of the tunnel would still be there, but, to his horror, it had been moved. Nowhere was it to be found.

He explained his dilemma. The wicked witch, Silba,

Flipper Green Frog.

must be responsible for this magical phenomenon. A rock can't move by itself, can it now?" said Billy while scratching his head.

"Oh, but it can. The wicked witch can do anything she likes," croaked the frog.

"Anything?" butted in Alberta.

"Oh, yes, anything you like. She's a dab hand at making things fly around in mid-air. One day it was raining cats and dogs, and the next she had flooded the forest completely – not a person to get all tangled up with, I can tell you. She is always ranting and raving, chanting and craving. Diddley pop, diddley flop, and how's your Aunt Annie? She is always annoying and criticising. She makes a new broomstick every day, and tests it out by flying with her magical cat, named Zuppy, unaided through the sky at night, especially after the midnight hour. Am I frightening you, children?" exclaimed Mr Frog.

"Oh, no. Do tell us more," cried out all the children at once.

Grandma Chadwick butted in abruptly, and told the children that they just didn't have time to squander. They just had to quickly find a new tunnel to explore.

Billy led the way as usual, followed by Arthur and Bella, who were hobbling along with their walking sticks. Then behind the grandparents was Mr Frog, followed by all the excited children.

It wasn't long before they all heard the familiar sound of "Quack! Quack! Quack!"

Suzanne quickly declared, "That sounds like a duck, if I'm not mistaken."

"Oh, bravo!" chuckled everyone else.

And, to their amazement, it was a duck – a lost duck. "Oh, are you friends, or are you foes?" asked the duck hesitantly.

"Oh, we are friends of the animal world. We are not here to harm you, Mr Duck, but to guide you safely home again."

Well, the duck cried a river of tears, and mumbled out his name. "My name's Frederick – Frederick the duck, from Nottingham. I suppose I'd better tell you my story."

"Oh, please do, Mr Duck. We would all like to know."

"Well, one day while I was swimming along on a calm lazy day on the river, minding my own business, I decided to swim past the tall green reeds and white water lilies. I dived underneath the water to see what fish were down there, but, on this day, I swam down and down too far for a duck like me to travel. And – this is no lie, young man – all of a sudden the riverbed, sand, silt and mud parted and I was sucked down through what I can only describe as a giant whirlpool to this place which we are all standing in. When I gathered my senses and looked around, guess what? There was no blue sky, no white fluffy clouds, no green grass or any other thing worth mentioning. And, ever since, I've been trudging and wandering around here in this silly cold damp tunnel. I'm like a maddened duck, in a frustrating maze with no way out, seemingly, my friends. I do meet other creatures down here, who are also lost. To be lost is a great misadventure, young man; and now it seems you'll be lost too if you venture too far away from wherever you came from."

"Not if I can help it, we won't," said Billy angrily.

"There must be a solution to our problem," shouted out Joe, the second youngest child. "I don't want to die down here in this smelly dank atmosphere. Where is the witch, Silba, and that rascal Slobber Dom, Dom and his sidekick, Jingle Black Jack? If they were here I'd leather the lot of them," cried out little Joe.

Now the frog was in deep thought, contemplating something. "What is it, Mr Flipper Frog? Do you have an idea? I do hope so, because both ends of the tunnel have now been bricked and blocked up," implored Samantha.

"Oh, I am thinking hard. That's it! I have a idea, if my

memory serves me well. I am trying to think of all the chants and spells that the witch uses most frequently. Yes, I have it."

"Have what?" exclaimed Bella Chadwick.

"I think it goes like this: Lushy, Rushy, Tushy. Or is it Rattle, Battle, Tattle? Or maybe it's Boranium, Foranium, Daranium."

"What on earth are you talking about, Mr Frog?" questioned Arthur Chadwick, bent over his walking cane.

"Look, everybody, the walls have gone – no bricks to be seen anywhere. Come, everybody, let's make good our escape before who knows what might happen next," shouted Billy excitedly.

They all ran along, except for Arthur and his wife, who were exhausted from their ordeal. Their legs just would not carry them far.

"Why, thank you, Mr Frog, for you have saved the day, and miraculously your chant has made a remarkable dent in the witch's cruel clandestine methods," said Alberta reassuringly.

Chapter Three

King Christopher and His Queen

With great fortitude, they all made it safely and found themselves back with the ant colony, where Christopher the king ant was in attendance. "My, oh my, what do we have here, then? Let me count. Seven humans, a duck and a frog, and is it Peter, you say, who is in your glass jar?"

"That's right, Christopher, a long chain of people and animals who are all exhausted from their grievances and misfortunes of one kind or another," said Billy dolefully.

"Well, I suppose I'll have to look after everyone and see to it that you are all fed with good wholesome food, and find you all beds to sleep on. I have the perfect solution. We have plenty of honey, which the bees have so kindly donated to us, and we have plenty of fruits of all kinds down here, so nobody will go without. You'll come to my banqueting table as my special guests, and we will talk later of what we can do for you," replied Christopher enthusiastically.

Soon all the wonderful worker ants were ferrying food and other items in a never-ending column around the maze of tunnels and large caves, preparing everything on the orders of their helpful monarch, Christopher the King of the Ants.

Everyone felt so pleased and safe, knowing that good

fortune had at last smiled on them all. And after an afternoon's rest, lying on large green and brown leaves, everyone awoke to the beautiful aroma of food, which was slowly being cooked for them by all the tired worker ants.

Soon it was six o'clock in the evening. The big gong was sounded for the approach of supper, and everyone was taken to the largest banqueting hall they had ever seen. There were large blue and gold curtains, with painted stars on them, flowing from roof to floor. And there was the longest dining table, made from oak and chestnut, with fine silverware, ceramic plates and cutlery, and large chandeliers hanging down from the high ceilings, with an assortment of different-coloured candles, now lit and glowing hot, fit for a king or queen to be seated at. They all sat down on large wooden chairs, with purple cloth seats, which were striped with golden silk inlays. Giant bumblebees and wasps, with fluorescent wings, darted and glided smoothly across the dining table, bringing with them sweet nectar and honeypots, allowing each guest his own set place at the magnificent table.

Then trumpets could be heard, and the trumpeters with their golden banners walked through and stood to attention behind the bemused guests. King Christopher now entered the great hall with his queen.

Queen Maybelene had not been seen for over a year, because she had been peacefully asleep whilst her army of worker ants constructed her a befitting kingdom to be proud of. Everywhere throughout her great palace were giant crystals of pink, white, blue, red, orange, purple and yellow – all the magic colours of the rainbow – illuminated with light beams, shining and reflecting. She was a gorgeous queen ant, and she and the King looked splendid when they walked to the opposite ends of the banqueting table.

One lone trumpeter now sounded his golden trumpet with great reverence as the two monarchs sat down.

King Christopher then stood, and clapped his hands

and said to everyone there, "Be happy, be merry, and enjoy the occasion. It's not every day a king ant meets his queen for the first time. So enjoy with enthusiasm, and I welcome you, my wife, Queen Honeypot Maybelene, the future heir and custodian of the ant kingdom."

Everyone tucked into their delicious food with helpings of magical ingredients and sauces, which no humans could ever make. They all made many beautiful comments in the direction of the Queen, showering her with delightful words.

Billy rose and bowed towards Her Majesty with great pomp and aplomb, and he could see that King Christopher acknowledged him with a bow of his head and a smile in his deep-blue eyes.

Bella and Arthur Chadwick were overwhelmed by all the niceties, and the good treatment that they were experiencing. They watched with joy in their hearts whilst the children were somewhat mesmerised by the whole affair.

Meanwhile, Flipper the frog amazed everyone when he suddenly blew up into a large bulbous overgrown frog of immense size, and exploded with a burp that astonished everyone. It made the Queen blush somewhat, and some smaller ants were blown across the room.

Flipper became embarrassed whilst he released more gases from his gaping mouth, pleasantly burping all the more. The laughter and giggles became so infectious that the whole of the court laughed until they had stitches in their stomachs, and they fell about with tears streaming down their faces.

Christopher the king ant settled everyone and bade them to keep good manners whilst at the dining table, and he came up with a plan of action so as to help the Chadwick family out of their dilemma. "Firstly, I will take you all tomorrow at first light to the tunnel entrance of Blackbird Wood and see you safely from these mazes which, as you know, are strictly for insects only. But, because I am king down here, I make the

"I Am the King
and I Make the Rules."

rules in accordance with our customary laws. It has been a pleasure having you all here at my command, and you will always be welcome if you find yourselves in any other trouble. Tonight you shall sleep peacefully for tomorrow's adventure, which surely will entertain you. Life is one big mystery, and you must be all strong within your hearts if you wish to succeed. I am well aware of the dangers of the forest, especially when you have creatures and demons, such as Slobber Dom, Dom and the wicked witch Silba, wandering around like fools at the garden fête. Leave them to their own silly devices and you will remain unhurt. One fine day, Nature with all her wisdom will surely catch these mischievous persons out and teach them a good lesson. What goes around comes around. Remember my words and pay attention to everyone you meet in Blackbird Wood. Not everyone is a friend, as you may believe them to be. There are those who are just waiting for you to fall into their wicked traps, with deception and betrayal. You must learn now and quickly, especially for when you next meet Jingle Black Jack. He is the most ruthless of cats. So don't take him at his word, for he means business every time."

Later on, after enjoying a night's entertainment in song and dance, the Chadwick family went to bed early, and dreamed of many fanciful things.

Alberta woke first and wiped the sleep from her green eyes. She picked up the glass bottle with Peter inside, and spoke to him of her intentions. She promised him she would do everything within her power to transform him back again into a fine gentleman, and he was not to lose hope, but have faith and courage, and survive his ordeal. But no answer came from Peter – for all the world he was just another beautiful butterfly, with similar colours to that of a red admiral. She put in some lettuce and flower petals, hoping the interned insect would at least try to eat something. It must be horrible to be a captive, where there is nowhere to go, just flying around aimlessly inside a circular prison.

Now Frederick the duck rose from his peaceful sleep and quacked himself awake. He plucked at his fine green, brown, blue and white feathers, whilst washing himself down.

"Don't you ever get fed up, Mr Duck, being just a duck?" enquired Alberta.

"Oh, no, because I'm a handsome duck, and I have plenty of things to do – when I am not trapped in a cave, that is."

"Well then, we'll be free soon enough, Frederick. The day is new and we have a lot to do. So dress yourself and be ready with the rest of us. I'll go and shake Mr Frog now and see if his large stomach has gone down," spoke Alberta excitedly.

Eventually all the children and adults gathered themselves and had a quick breakfast in the quiet dining room. Christopher came and told them to meet him in one hour.

At the appointed time, the King of the Ants, with the aid of his marcher ants, now got everybody in line and marched them to the entrance, which was some three miles away.

When they all finally arrived, the morning sun had risen in the east, and its beautiful rays penetrated down the shaft inside the tunnel. Everyone clambered out easily, except for Arthur and Bella Chadwick, who were unable to do things on their own. But help came from Billy, who passed them down a rope which he had in his haversack, and they were soon pulled from their enclosure safely and in one piece.

Everyone thanked Christopher, King of the Ants, for his hospitality and protection. He suggested that they follow a route to the west of Blackbird Wood, where eventually they should find their way back through the forest and back home to safety. They all walked away waving goodbye to the ant colony and its majestic king.

The walk was tiring and seemingly never-ending. They walked over rocks and inclines, down steep slopes and up embankments which were steep and wet in places. They slashed their way through thick vegetation and large green ferns that they'd never seen before. They stopped occasionally, giving their grandparents rest and water.

It was nearly midday when they came across a large clearing with hundreds of mushrooms, bluebells, daisies, buttercups and other wild plants, which were like a beautiful carpet covering the whole of the wooded area. Massive oak, elm, ash, and cedar trees grew up through the clouds to a blue backdrop of different hues and other marvellous colours. They all stood in amazement and took in the beautiful scenery. Cuckoos, thrushes, robins, blackbirds, blue and yellow tits and other fascinating creatures of the air, were all singing and warbling to each other. Large deer and stags, after being startled, jumped and darted over wild shrubs and plants to escape back into the darkness of the forest. There was a ghostly feel to the woods. When the birds occasionally stopped singing, you could hear a pin drop it was so quiet.

Suddenly, from the undergrowth, a wild boar came darting out like a ferocious mad lion and charged straight at Billy Chadwick, who was the leader of the team. Everyone scattered, hiding behind trees for protection, whilst Billy fought wildly, using the long walking stick that he had made from a piece of ash wood he'd found along the route. He struck the beast several times about the body, causing it to scamper away howling with pain. He was lucky to survive the ordeal. The wild boar had scraped Billy's left leg badly along the calf. Alberta dressed his wounds with a strip of cloth torn from his own shirt.

The frog and the duck were terrified, and hid themselves underneath a large fallen oak tree, too frightened to speak. They eventually came from their

A Real Leprechaun.

temporary hideaway and croaked and quacked for some considerable time, shaking with complete fear.

Billy took charge again and tried desperately to calm everyone down, especially the girls.

Samantha, the youngest child, was crying, with large silver tears running down her red-blossomed cheeks. "If only we could go home," she cried out miserably. "I don't like the forest one bit, I don't," she continued.

"We must all be strong – stronger than I thought. We must stay together as a tight-knit group and challenge our fears, fight on and conquer the dark void of the forest!" exclaimed Billy Chadwick boldly.

They continued on all afternoon, plodding along, seemingly going around and around in circles. The little remaining light flickered through the treetops, dancing like shadows, making weird shapes across the vegetation and ground.

Suddenly they heard a voice shout out, seemingly from nowhere in particular: "Are ye lost in Blackbird Wood?" The voice came again, slightly echoing through the woods: "Maybe I can help ye from your dilemma."

Arthur Chadwick pushed his way forward and poked around with his walking stick, pushing away the giant tree branches in front of him, and there, to his astonishment, was a green and red leprechaun, sat cross-legged on top of a giant white and red toadstool, smoking a wooden pipe. "Come, everyone, and follow me. We seem to have a remarkable customer right here in the middle of the forest," said Arthur.

"What on earth do you mean, Arthur?" enquired Bella Chadwick excitedly.

"Look, over there." Arthur pointed.

Everyone pushed and shoved for a better view.

"Oh, my God, a real leprechaun – at least I think it is," said Bella Chadwick again.

They all hurried themselves and went through to where the smiling sprite sat alone. He sported a red pointed hat, which had tiny brass bells on the end, and he had a long white beard.

"Top of the morning to ye, sir. I'm Sniggy Bells, the famous leprechaun of Blackbird Wood. And what can I be doing for ye all on this bright late afternoon? If it's me mother ye want to talk to, I only have to whistle, ye know, and she'll appear with her golden wand. Dubbly de dubbly de. The top of the morning to ye all. Ireland's a long ways off from here and I'm having trouble getting back over the terrible Irish Sea. Ye know, between England and Ireland there is another magical island, named the Isle of Man, that faraway Viking rock where all the fairies hide underneath the fairy bridge of time. I'm lost, I tell ye, for ever and ever, except for Jingle Black Jack, of course. Forgive me if I seem rather rude with me explanations," declared the leprechaun as he babbled on and on in some kind of foreign dialect, seemingly in a world of his own.

Everyone present froze with sheer terror when they heard those three sinister words, Jingle Black Jack.

"What on earth is the matter with everyone? Have I said something wrong?" declared the leprechaun. "Let me think – is it Irish gibberish? Or is it a bizarre word that I have let slip from me mouth, which won't stop talking?" he continued.

"Oh, Mr Leprechaun, we were so scared when you mentioned Jingle Black Jack. He is a wretched black creature of the forest – a demon, in fact," cried out Suzanne and Joe together.

"Oh, you must be mistaken – he's only a friendly harmless pussycat. From what I've seen, he is kind and helpful – not the cat that you describe."

"Oh, but you must believe us. He and his master, Slobber Dom, Dom, have already created havoc, almost destroying our beautiful house, Buttercup Cottage, and we are now all homeless and lost like your good self, Mr Leprechaun," said little Miss Samantha worriedly.

"And who is Slobber Dom, Dom, must I ask? A very queer name to have, don't you think?" invited the leprechaun. He shook and shook his pipe upside down several times while they were talking, and relit it afterwards. "To be lost is a miserable thing, and especially in a large forest like this one – not a happy position to be in."

"Oh, please do stop it, Mr Leprechaun. We are being serious with our disclosures. Stop this charade and your philosophical nonsense at once," cried out Frederick the duck, almost in despair from listening to the leprechaun's twiddle-twaddle.

Billy now intervened and asked the leprechaun where Jingle Black Jack was. Had he disappeared from view? Had he gone home?

"Oh, Jingle Black Jack is out hunting deep in the forest of Blackbird Wood. Who knows what he is up to. Maybe he is being helpful, ye know, carrying wood for some old haggard spinster, or he could be taking someone's children to the schoolhouse in the local village. Oh what a beautiful purring cat he is!" invented the smiling leprechaun.

"That is a load of tripe, and you know it is, Mr Leprechaun," fumed Billy Chadwick.

"Oh, I wish ye would call me by me proper title, Sniggy Bells." He continued: "If ye all follow that path down there to the right of your position, it will lead ye to safety, rest and food, where many beautiful things will happen to ye all." With that last statement, Sniggy Bells disappeared in a cloud of smoke.

Everyone was astonished with what had just happened. Was he telling them the truth? Was he another evil sprite come to mislead them on their peculiar journey through the woods?

"I don't believe a word he has said!" exclaimed Arthur Chadwick.

"But we can't stay here, can we? We must move on quickly before night falls," cried out little Joe, aged seven.

"And it's getting very cold indeed," shouted Suzanne fearfully.

Chapter Four

Trojan the Troll

So they all went on, following the leprechaun's advice. The route they had chosen was a very long winding path, which took them deeper and deeper into the woods.

They eventually came across a clearing, and before their very eyes was the most beautiful place they'd ever seen. A large glittering waterfall was flowing down with much splash over the top of a gigantic rock and into a deep blue and green pool, where water-lily pads and reeds were in abundance. Beside the pool was a plateau, with a circumference of about eighty feet, surrounded by beautiful weeping willows and trees whose names were not known to them.

There was a hidden cave underneath the waterfall that Billy Chadwick soon discovered with so much glee in his heart. He shouted to the rest of his tired troop that it was safe to come across and inspect his new find.

They all settled down for the night and lit a raging fire. Food was in abundance; everywhere they looked were apples, oranges, pears, figs, bananas, dates, cucumbers, potatoes, carrots, lettuces, cabbages, plums, grapes, peas, onions, lemons, grapefruit, asparagus, corn, wheat, barley, and other delicious varieties of fruits and beautiful trees which filled the immediate area around the cave and waterfall. It was like some kind of tropical paradise. But how could this be in an English forest?

Later, when they had gathered in all of their provisions, Billy Chadwick decided to explore the cave complex further. He had discovered a network of tunnels that ran from the depths of the cave.

Ten minutes later, Billy Chadwick suddenly froze, unable to help himself, for there ahead of him was a huge pile of what looked like white and grey animal bones. They were piled right to the top of the roof. Fraught with fear and foreboding he dreaded the worst. Around the bend he saw human skulls and skeletons.

'What am I to do now?' thought Billy Chadwick. 'If I disclose my find to the others, they will surely panic and flee into the unknown again.'

He checked all about him to see if any other horrors might be hidden thereabouts, but there was nothing more that he could perceive. So he turned and fled back to the others, and kept his horrendous secret to himself for the time being.

Everyone was so tired after they had eaten their scrumptious food and fruit. Even the frog and duck were extremely happy with their good fortune at the last hour of the day.

Billy joined the others and found a place to sleep around the fire. Throughout the night they all snored loudly, except for Billy Chadwick, who was half awake. Every now and then he would open one eye to see if anything mischievous was afoot, fearing a wild beast or a lion might come back to its lair. 'How silly!' he thought. 'A lion? Lions don't live in England!' Then he dozed off again.

Everyone was so tired that they all slept longer than usual.

Suddenly the cave complex shuddered greatly, and there was a noise like the sound of thunder. The rock face shook and a few stones and rocks fell about them. It felt as though the earth itself had come apart at the seams.

With the deafening sound of thud, thud, thud, the duck and frog became most terrified and hid themselves alongside Arthur and Bella Chadwick. Flipper the frog hid underneath Bella's skirt, hoping he would be protected.

The noise finally stopped just as quickly as it had arrived. Just silence and a eerie ambiance remained.

Suddenly a loud harsh voice echoed thereabouts. "Who is sleeping and eating in my cave, then? Come out, you who trespass in my domain. I know you are in there, because I can smell you, and I shall eat you alive if you don't come out. I am very hungry indeed," said the dreadful voice.

What were they to do now? Seemingly they were all in a trap, with no way out at all.

Billy Chadwick clasped his hands tightly together and shouted from the top of his lungs, "Who is it? Who commands such things? Are you a beast of the woods? What is your name, stranger?" continued Billy.

"I am a monster troll who orders these things. And I will club you all to death with my huge wooden stick. I know there is a lot of you in my cave, so come out now and face me square on. My name is Trojan the troll of Blackbird Wood," shouted out the troll convincingly.

"Are these bones that I have found, human and animal, bones that you have eaten previously?" declared Billy heroically.

"Yes, they are, and, my dear friend, you will be the next unfortunate victim on my large menu. So come out and be brave before you die on my big dinner plate," shouted out the troll menacingly.

The bad troll swung his large wooden bludgeon underneath the raging waterfall, trying his best to dislodge the Chadwick family. But it was no use, because the family retreated back into the cave complex.

This annoyed the bad troll very much indeed. "I will come in soon and consume you all, because I am very tired indeed."

The One-Eyed Troll of
Blackbird Wood.

All the girls, boys, animals and Bella Chadwick became hysterical at just the mention of being eaten alive.

Billy now made a courageous plea to the mighty troll. "Please, please, I beg of you not to eat us alive. We are not trespassers, as you think we are. We came here because we are lost and frightened, and there was nowhere else to go until we discovered this beautiful place in Blackbird Wood."

"Oh, did you now? Not a very wise choice, is it, to fall upon a troll's home? How would you like it if I came and slept in your place of residence?" bellowed the troll.

"Yes, I must agree with you. You do have a point to this terrifying argument," said Billy Chadwick apprehensively.

With that, Billy came up with a daring plan. "It might just work," he told everyone. He then went to work and made a large lasso from the rope he carried. He took it to the cave entrance and made the rope as inconspicuous as possible beside a rock.

The big bad troll exploded again. "Do I smell a duck and a slimy frog in there? That is my speciality. Who would believe it? a roasted duck for my supper – one that I can digest easily."

"Okay, Trojan the troll, the game's up and we're all coming out bravely to face whatever consequence it may bring us," said Billy alarmingly.

Billy boldly went first, tying the other end of his rope to his right hand, which he placed in his trouser pocket. He led the way carefully, with everyone else following behind in a column of fearful human beings.

The bad troll was cheerful indeed. At last he had coaxed them from his lair. When they had all assembled, the troll swung his dangerous club at them. With all his might he swung it from side to side, but he was out of reach by a good two feet, which made him very angry indeed. He huffed and he puffed with such noise that the ground vibrated all the more. He had also, in his mad dash, trampled most of the beautiful trees which were in his path and squashed fruits and vegetables lay in a messy mush of smelly juices. The one-eyed troll moved around in circles, mashing more fruits underneath his enormous feet, while Billy walked further away from the entrance, dodging every move the troll made.

Luckily the troll fell into Billy's trap. His left foot stood momentarily in the lasso noose, and Billy pulled quickly, tripping the massive troll over onto the ground. He came crashing down upon the earth and lake with an almighty splash and with such powerful force that the earth rocked violently.

For some considerable time the troll lay in his own crater, which was very wide and deep, and water splashed on his half-buried face.

Everyone, except for Billy, scrambled away from the giant troll while he lay unconscious, murmuring unintelligible words: "Humble, bumble, tumble, rumble. Is it some kind of trick. Humble, bumble, tumble, rumble. Please don't make me sick."

All the boys and girls now helped Billy to pull away the giant club which the troll still held tightly in his palm.

Suzanne went and tickled the monster troll underneath his armpit with a large wooden stick, so as to loosen his powerful grip.

After three agonising minutes the troll gave in, and they were able to free the club and drag it safely away.

Billy walked up and down on top of the monster troll like a victorious general on the battlefield, whilst the children tied his legs together so he could not walk properly.

Suddenly the troll started to wake. He sneezed violently, sending Billy flying through the air and into the pool, where he landed safely. Everyone thought this was highly amusing. And Frederick the duck quacked and quacked until he was tired of it.

The troll awoke from his deep sleep all dishevelled

and wet from his good soaking. He could not help himself any more. The bang on his head had made him forgetful and disorientated.

Little Joe and Samantha tickled the troll's big ugly nose with a large white duck feather until he couldn't stand it any longer. He sneezed and sneezed greatly indeed, sending everyone for cover each time he did so.

The children kept on teasing the unfriendly giant by speaking through his hairy ears: "Oh, you are a naughty big troll, are you not? What big feet you have! And they smell too of an odour I have never smelt before. A one-eyed troll? Hey, not so clever, are we now?"

They all sat on the troll's large overgrown belly, which was going up and down every time he breathed in and out, and they wondered what they were going to do next.

"Do we kill the troll?" enquired Bella Chadwick.

"Oh no, we mustn't do that, because life is so precious, even if he is a mean bad old troll," said Billy wisely.

The troll just lay there, grunting and groaning until he finally came to his senses. "Help me up at once," cried the troll. He continued: "If you don't, I will smash you all to pieces in one go."

"Still threatening us, are you?" answered brave Billy.

"This is my proposal, Trojan the troll. If you make a promise to yourself not to eat or harm us, then we will let you go. Now, we can't be fairer than that, can we?" said Arthur Chadwick, whilst prodding the giant troll in his ribcage with his walking stick.

After a few minutes the troll replied, "I promise faithfully not to do any wicked things to you all, and I will become a friendly giant instead."

With that, young Joe and Billy went and untied the rope which was bound tightly around the troll's legs.

Everyone drew back and waited anxiously whilst the troll kicked and kicked his legs, trying hard to find his grip on the ground. After five long minutes the troll,

An Almighty Splash.

half submerged, got to his feet and stood there with a few tears rolling down his cheeks. Then he opened up his heart to the Chadwick family. "Please don't leave me here alone. Take me with you when you go. I've been a lonely troll for the past twenty years, and I'm rather fed up and miserable with my existence here in this large overgrown forest."

The Chadwick family began whispering amongst themselves, whilst the sad giant sat down on a giant tree trunk, and the ground shook violently as he did so. After lengthy discussions they all came to a suitable decision.

"Yes, after long consideration we have all decided you may come along with us on one condition. And that is that you will abide by our strict laws and customs, and help us if we get into any trouble," explained Billy Chadwick with a sense of authority in his voice.

"I accept, and I am very grateful for your friendship," cried the troll.

A shift in power had now gone to Billy Chadwick. With his strong leadership qualities he had made the giant creature kind and compliant to his authority. Billy had mastered the troll and had subdued his mighty appetite greatly.

Billy now gathered everyone together and stood proudly on top of a large flat rock. He spoke of their next great challenge. "We must all leave at once. Pick as many fruits and vegetables as you can for our long journey, and we will travel in a northerly direction by following the sun, which rises daily from the east. At night, if we are forced to, we will use the stars of heaven for our guidance. Do not worry. We have made it this far, so be confident and courageous, and conquer your doubts. We must all work as a team. A divided house cannot stand alone. We must unite and be brave like Alexander the Great, that great king from Macedonia."

Trojan the troll listened with great interest and said

that he would carry Bella, Arthur, Joe and Samantha Chadwick inside his giant leather satchel, which was slung across his large shoulders, so as to help them, because they were the oldest and youngest ones in the troop and they would not become exhausted on their frightening journey. So the huge troll bent down and carefully picked up those whom he had previously named.

Billy led the way, followed by Suzanne and Alberta, who carefully carried the glass jar containing Peter. The troll picked up his massive club and followed behind everyone else, and he seemed very happy to be led away from his lair.

After going some four miles through the forest, the troll became frantic. Something had scratched the back of his head severely as he went underneath a giant oak tree, and he screamed out in distress.

They stopped to investigate what was wrong with him.

"Who is in the trees of the forest? I smell a wicked creature afoot. What is your game? Come out from your hiding place at once!" groaned the troll.

There, up high in the branches, sat Jingle Black Jack with a vicious smile upon his face. With great mischief, and a sinister look in his yellow-and-black eyes, he just sat there spread along the branch, with one paw dangling.

"I knew it would not be long before we met you again, Jingle Black Jack. Up to our old tricks again, are we?" questioned Billy Chadwick.

"Are you all lost again? Can you not find your way out of this enchanted wood? Oh, what a shame that is for you all! I can help you, if you really desire it. You only have to ask me, and it shall be done.

"We don't need your help at all. We shall find our way from here back to Buttercup Cottage on our own, thank you very much," declared Alberta.

Jingle Black Jack purred and licked his evil claws,

then answered back, "Oh, what stupid human beings you all are! For I am the king of the jungle and forest around these parts," boasted the demon cat emphatically.

Meanwhile, Trojan wiped the trickle of blood from his head. He then licked his hand, and became angered by the wicked beast in the treetop. He began to brutally shake the tree, hoping to dislodge the large black cat of Blackbird Wood, but his efforts were no good.

Jingle Black Jack just fled, flying across to a distant tree, where seemingly he vanished for good.

So they carefully continued on their journey, keeping a lookout for Jingle Black Jack, who was a complete nuisance to everyone concerned. He was not the kind of cat you would take home to meet your mother. He was a displeasing cat who was damnable and disobedient at the best of times.

At last they emerged from the forest into a large valley. Luscious green fields lay on the horizon. Barley, wheat, rye and rape grew in abundance, and in the near distance were many high rolling hills and mountains which went as far and wide as the eye could see. It was a rather pleasant land to behold.

Billy checked that everyone was accounted for, and boldly led them through a glorious yellow rape field and on into a landscape of wheat fields.

'There must be a farmhouse or farmer out working his land somewhere,' they all thought together.

Herds of sheep, cattle and pigs could be seen and heard, with their constant bleating, mooing and grunting.

They went further, but there was no one to be found at all, which seemed rather puzzling.

Then, after three miles, they came across an old beggar, who appeared to be a tramp. He had a crooked stick, a black patch over his right eye, and his clothes were ragged and torn. He also carried a red canvas bag on the end of his stick, which was carried over his shoulder.

"Out walking, are we, strangers, good citizens of

Blackbird Wood? I've just had a sitting and consultation with Silba the witch in those mountains yonder. What a nice old lady she is! I'm so very happy because she said that I'm going to be rich beyond my wildest dreams. I've been travelling these woods for over fifty years, with just the birds for company," said the bearded tramp gleefully.

"Oh, it's nice to meet you. Do you have a given name?" asked Billy carefully.

"Oh, yes, they call me Lonesome Brian of Blackbird Wood."

They introduced themselves to the tramp, while carefully inspecting him to see if he was a cunning devil in disguise.

"Could you please direct us exactly to where Silba the witch lives and works?" asked Arthur Chadwick hopefully.

The tramp turned around and pointed in a north-easterly direction and told them all to get their fortunes told as they, too, might become rich.

Trojan moved his large wooden club right next to the travelling tramp's feet and roared, "I do hope you're telling us the truth, Brian of Blackbird Wood, because I don't like liars and folks who make up stories for the gullible to believe."

"Oh, I would never do a thing like that. I might be poor, but I'm as honest as the day is long," replied the fearful tramp.

So on they went, passing over a wide snaking river, which wasn't that deep. A few moments later Billy looked behind, and behold! there was no sign of the tramp. He had vanished as quickly as he had come?

About ten minutes later the Chadwick family came across some stone steps that led up a mountainside, and there on a signpost were the words 'Welcome to the Witch's Grotto of Blackbird Wood. Please enter at your own risk and follow the steps to have your fortunes told.'

Chapter Five

The Witch's Grotto

Everyone looked at one another rather puzzled, and apprehensively went up the many stone steps to the witch's den. There to their amazement was the witch's grotto with flashing colourful lights all over the place, and spelt out in green capital letters was the word 'GROTTO'.

Within the cave, before their very eyes, was Silba the witch, who was sitting down on a huge wooden chair beside an enormous spinning wheel, stirring with a large wooden ladle, inside what looked like a massive black cauldron, which was positioned on top of a large fire.

"Oh, cackle, rattle, tackle. Please bring me luck. Oh, cackle, rattle, tackle. Please bring me love. Oh, cackle, rattle, tackle. Please make me rich."

Everyone was astonished by the witch's chants and weird sayings. She was a typical witch, dressed in a black outfit with a black pointed hat. Warts and blemishes were on her wrinkled face. She had a huge hooked nose, black hairs protruded from her pointed chin below a sagging jaw and mouth, and obviously all her teeth were missing. An African baboon was sitting down on a large rock with a long leather lead fastened to its neck, eating and munching on a bunch of bananas.

Flipper the frog became agitated and jumped into the

nearby hedge to conceal himself.

The witch turned and waved an accusing finger at the group. "Are you weary travellers who are in need of a rest? I have the perfect remedy for that. Do you want your fortunes told by the Oracle of Double Bubble? Come and make yourself known to Silba the witch of Blackbird Wood. There's nothing that I cannot do. I can make a loved one return. I can do all manner of secret tricks. The moon and stars is my favourite chant. Even the weather I command with a flick of my magic stick. Come into my grotto and gaze into my crystal ball – for a few pennies, of course. Do I smell a giant toad amongst you? What a big friend you have – a roaming troll. I hope he is not a dangerous one. Come, and tell me all your innocent desires and deepest wishes too."

Billy told the witch of their adventure and misfortunes in Blackbird Wood and their daring escapes.

The witch listened carefully and smiled cunningly at Billy's mishaps. She declared, "I am the seventh child from a roaming family of gypsies, and I can make you all rich beyond your wildest dreams. Look over there – in my great chest of magic you will find a suitable talisman, charms and written chants for your every wish. Is it trinkets of gold and silver that you wish for? Or do you wish for a genie to appear from his magic lamp? I can provide everything for all your needs," continued the witch in confident style.

But Frederick the duck was having none of the witch's promises. "What a load of baloney you talk, Silba the witch. You're nothing but a con woman out for a fine catch from unsuspecting travellers. You can't fool me or my comrades with all your foolish nonsense. It's all double Dutch, gibberish and babble. I could tell my own fortune in seconds. We're all lost and tired, and that's the end of that. If you're that clever, turn me into a wolf."

"You've asked for it, duck. What you wish for is my command. "Chuckle, buckle, duckle," declared the witch, and, with three more chants, poor old Frederick was changed into a benevolent wolf.

"Change him back into a duck immediately," shouted out Alberta daringly and expectantly.

"Oh, but I can't, because the spell has to be reversed, which is always a complicated thing to do – not as easy as you think," cackled the witch. She continued: "What I really need is a big fat juicy frog or toad, so as to transform the duck back into his natural form. The frog I once knew and owned has taken flight and escaped my notice. I'm really sorry about all that. I'm an old woman now, past her sell-by date, don't you think? I could use the tarot cards to see if his future is a bright one, or a dark one. Who knows? he might be happy being a wolf – one who can roam the forest freely. Who in their right mind would like to be a duck who quacks all day long, with no respite coming? If you all stay here with me tonight, I will make your visit well worth it. I've got plenty of surprises in store for you all."

With that, the Chadwick family all came inside the witch's grotto, where all manner of things were on show. Many different eyes stared back at them from the back of the cave, and they were startled somewhat by the sound of a multitude of stray wild black cats, who howled and screeched their annoyance at being invaded by the Chadwick family, as they darted out of the way.

Also to be found were great chests of gold and silver, precious jewels such as sapphires, rubies and diamonds, and other treasures and artefacts. These intrigued the tired family, especially the youngest children, who could not stop touching things.

"Oh, do be careful, you just might disappear for good. Who knows what might happen in Blackbird Wood? Caution is the best policy in the world. Don't touch things that don't belong to you. That's my motto when one is in my grotto. So abide by my rules, little ones.

"What I Really Need Is a
Big Fat Juicy Frog."

Then you'll be all right, won't you?" said Silba in a frightening manner.

The baboon began to snarl, showing his ferocious teeth. Whilst jumping up and down he threw a banana skin at Samantha, who stepped back from the onslaught and naughtiness.

"Can't you control that monkey of yours, Silba? It's out of control, with a menacing dark look in its eyes," said Bella Chadwick.

"Oh, Saladin is all right when you get to know him. He's just a little tired and agitated right now," declared the witch slyly.

Silba now began making a suitable passageway through all the junk and mess of the grotto. Then she wiped her large table clean with a sweep of her arm, moving off all of her magic papers, designs, stars and other curiosities, leaving only a black surface that had a six-pointed star painted on the tabletop with an array of golden stars at each corner. On the front, where she seated herself, was her magical crystal ball.

"Oh, come, all who are demoralised, and be seated at the Oracle of Double Bubble, where I will see and scribe your futures with precision and accuracy."

Meanwhile, Flipper the frog was so fed up with himself, whilst hiding in the undergrowth outside, that he was getting very lonely indeed. But he could not venture too far, because of the witch's wrath and her acute senses in detecting him. He was scared of being used again in her rituals, rites and silly remedies. So he stayed by himself, out of harm's way, to wait until the Chadwick family left the grotto for good.

Trojan the troll also sat outside the cave entrance, biding his time in boredom. He listened to the old hag, who seemed quite happy with herself, talking constantly about what she could achieve with her wild chants and magical rites, which he thought were a load of old codswallop. On and on she went, babbling in all sorts of foreign dialects, like a wizard gone wrong. Also, because of his size, he could not fit easily inside the den at all, so he waited patiently, guarding the entrance of the grotto.

Apprehensively, the Chadwick family seated themselves as requested by the witch of Blackbird Wood.

First to have a reading were Arthur and Bella Chadwick.

"Are you comfortable? Then I shall begin," said the witch. "I see a great fortune, hundreds of pounds, silver and gold. All will be well with you both. You will have great happiness, and your health will improve tremendously. So eat plenty of honey and jam. That is all that I see for you both at this present time. Who is next, may I ask politely?"

In came Joe, Billy, Samantha, Suzanne and Alberta, all full of giggles as they all sat down around her large table, expecting a good reading.

"Oh, cackle, cackle," said the witch alarmingly. She paused for a second or two. "Oh, let me see as I scribe the waters. Oh, yes! There are numerous challenges and different trials to go through until you find perfect happiness here within the forest of Blackbird Wood. Only with your intelligence will you be able to be free of pain and heartache."

With that, Zuppy, her magical cat, jumped upon the table, scattering all the witch's magical aids about the place, which infuriated Silba. She removed the offender by sending her cat through the air with her left hand. Then Saladin screeched in a high-pitched voice as he jumped into the shadows of the grotto away from his mistress's wrath and torment.

"Get out of my way, you blithering cat. Oh, I do apologise, children. Zuppy has got a problem, a mighty problem – being nosey, whilst interfering with my readings. I cannot do a reading with animals who do not do as they are told," laboured the old witch. She now gazed into her crystal ball. "Oh, come, children, don't be disappointed. I have many surprises in store for you. I can see much adventure and distress as you travel in Blackbird Wood. But there is danger and excitement. You'll have to be on your toes – on guard, as one might say," warned Silba.

"But what about riches, luck and prosperity?" shouted out Joe excitedly.

"Riches, health, luck and happiness. Everyone wants to know about these things, young man. Half the problem is that in reality we make our own luck by thinking correctly and by making careful choices. If you all survive, then I can see good things happening to you all," advised Silba soothingly.

"If we survive?" asked Billy attentively.

"Yes, children, because there are dark forces in the woods – bad spirits that love to do pranks and cause mischief. They are impostors who know how to change their appearance at will."

"At will?" asked Samantha carefully.

"Yes, children, with the will of the devil. Who knows? I might even be a bad spirit, before your very eyes. Do you trust me like one of your own?" questioned the cunning witch further.

"Oh, yes, Silba. At the moment we have no reason to doubt you. Your kind hospitality shows rightly enough that you are a good caring witch," replied Alberta wisely.

"Well, then, if by any chance you come across a mighty frog, named Flipper Green Roger, I will be pleased, because he has gone astray, being a naughty frog to boot. You don't know where he is, do you, children? I will pay handsomely if you can find him for me," announced the witch carefully. And with that Silba bade them goodbye.

Outside the grotto, Trojan the troll picked up Arthur and Bella Chadwick and placed them carefully inside his leather pouch. They prepared themselves for the upcoming journey.

The witch had directed them north, across a

Trojan Picked up Arthur and
Bella Chadwick.

mountainous rocky region, which would take them back to Buttercup Cottage.

Being wise, Billy picked up Flipper Green Roger quickly and concealed him within the inside pocket of his blue jacket. He hoped that the witch would not become aware of his hidden secret.

Frederick the wolf howled aloud as they all walked on into the unknown realms of Blackbird Wood.

With Billy Chadwick leading the way, they climbed and climbed upwards across uneven terrain, until they found a winding path which sheep and mountain goats had used over the centuries. With the midday sun burning brightly in between the white fluffy clouds they arrived at a large plateau which wound around the mountain edge. There was a mighty drop of thousands of feet into an abyss far, far below.

As they went on, small rocks underneath their feet started to fall away from the mountain edge and they all clung on to the mountainside. Eventually they came to a large ravine which could only be crossed by an old wood-and-rope bridge that wobbled in the wind from side to side.

All the girls in the troop were clearly frightened. More stones fell over the side as they walked precariously on, and nobody could hear the rocks and stones hit the bottom of the deep crevasse; it was like a bottomless pit.

Trojan could not go across the bridge owing to his immense size. Nor could he jump across, it being about 100 feet wide. The only way for him was to climb down, and find another route across the raging river far below.

Billy said that he would go first over the old bridge to test it out before allowing the others to proceed. He told Trojan to find his own way down and across the river, accompanied by Arthur and Bella Chadwick, and they would all meet up later.

After testing the swinging bridge, Billy came back and told Joe to take all the girls across with him, hand in hand, which he did successfully, and Frederick the wolf followed them.

Then it was Billy's turn. Braving the elements, brave Billy Chadwick was halfway across when he looked behind. Slobber Dom, Dom and his evil black cat were standing there cutting through the thick vines which fastened the bridge to their side of the ravine. With nowhere to run, Billy held on with all his might. As the vines gave way the bridge swung across to the other side of the mountain pass. Billy was left hanging on fifty feet below his frightened family.

Jingle Black Jack snarled ferociously in triumph with his paw dangling over the side of the ravine as Slobber Dom, Dom congratulated him for his cunningness.

As Billy held on, all his family encouraged him to climb back up the broken bridge to safety and away from the two evil offenders. They wondered if Silba the witch had also been involved in this terrible deed. It was anybody's guess. She liked meddling with danger and had a bad attitude.

Billy began to climb up, clutching at the rope for support. He was tired and annoyed at the two bad instigators of mischief. Although in distress from his painful ordeal, Billy felt lucky to be alive as he scrambled over the top of the ravine onto the mountain ridge. When they looked back, to everyone's astonishment, Slobber Dom, Dom and his sidekick had fled away into invisible realms. It was as if it was a bad dream they had experienced.

Chapter Six

The Fairy Kingdom

After giving Billy a hero's welcome back and ten minutes' rest, the family gathered themselves. With Billy once again leading from the front they marched on, keeping close together as they went down the mountain pass. An hour later they met up again with Trojan, Arthur and Bella Chadwick. Trojan was mad when he heard about the well-prepared ambush by the two devious sprites when Billy could have been killed if it had not been for his audacious bravery. After three hours of trekking though the wilderness they came to a clearing where there were exotic plants and thousands of different mushrooms – some spotted, some striped, some with colourful patterns, and some as big as houses.

Suddenly a voice was heard, and to everyone's amazement Sniggy Bells was sat on top of a large toadstool in deep contemplation whilst smoking his large black pipe.

"Oh, we all meet again. What a coincidence that is! Are ye all still lost, like going around and around in a maze? I hear that your old pal Slobber Dom, Dom is up to his old tricks once more. News travels fast when one is in the forest of Blackbird Wood."

"And how do you know that, then, country gnome?" challenged Billy as he rested upon his walking stick.

"Oh, it is as easy as one, two, three. The birds in the trees tell me what I wish to know. Any gossip and I'm the first to know. Oh, what a clever leprechaun I am to be filled with so much knowledge! A walking library is what I am around these parts. And for those naughty cunning sprites there will be a time when they're brought to answer for their crimes. Not very clever sprites, are they? Always trying to outdo us country folk," advised the leprechaun happily.

"Well, Mr Leprechaun, can you direct us back through Blackbird Wood to safety, seeing that you know everything there is to know?" asked brave Billy hopefully.

"Oh, that is a difficult question to ask of me, because sometimes I get all flabbergasted and forgetful. I used to live here. Where am I?" said the leprechaun.

"Why, Sniggy Bells, that doesn't make sense – not one bit of it. Not like the Queen's English, is it?" questioned Alberta, laughing as she did so.

"And if you do know, then it had better be true, full and precise," warned the troll as he tapped his hand with his giant club, threatening the leprechaun if he tried to trick them.

"Oh, there is no need for violence, my friend, for I am who I say I am – a trustworthy friend, especially to those who get lost in the dark fearsome woods." With that the confident leprechaun knocked his pipe empty, then he refilled it with new tobacco and lit it once more. "Ye only have to ask me kindly, and then I shall help ye find your way back from whence you came."

Frederick the wolf, who was once a duck, stretched his neck and howled, as if he knew that the leprechaun was telling the truth.

"If ye all go in a straight line, as the crow flies, for at least five miles, then turn due south, ye will come upon the magical fairy kingdom of Annatasia. I am sure that if ye behave yourselves, then the Fairy Queen, Theodora III, will help and support ye. She, and she alone, is the supreme fairy who governs fairly and correctly over her vast kingdom – the most beautiful benevolent fairy ye ever did see," advised Sniggy Bells confidently.

"Why, thank you, Sniggy Bells. One day we shall return the favour and help you if ever you get yourself into any trouble that you can't get out of."

As the Chadwicks discussed their position, the leprechaun disappeared from sight, as if he had never been there in the first place.

They all moved on again, walking at a fast pace in the direction given to them. After two hours they came across a signpost, which read:

THE KINGDOM OF ANNATASIA

Dear Traveller, Come and Rest and
Be Fed by Your Kind Hosts of
Blackbird Wood

Unbelievably, the landscape had changed to one of lush green fields, and in the far distance they could see a magnificent fortress, made from what looked like a million crystals. A spectrum of light shone brightly throughout its entire structure. Above were thousands of what looked like colourful balloons, all taking off and landing around the large city of crystal. Was it a surrealist dream? For how could it be? It was like nothing they had ever seen before in their entire lives. Was it a trick of the imagination, so planned by a bad sprite who knew of magical practices, invented to lure unsuspecting victims to their doom?

They rested and scanned the immediate horizon for anything else that was to be observed. Magic was now in the air. They, the Chadwicks, had been brought up on a daily diet of children's fairy tales, where there were lands of milk, honey and magic as in the storybooks of old.

After travelling for most of the day, they were all

A Magnificent Fortress.

quite weary. Led by the troll, they got closer to the beautiful crystal kingdom. Suddenly Trojan touched something that was strange, and he received a mild electric shock. The rest of the family also got a shock as they too went forward. Several times the family tried to go forward and the same thing happened. But how could this be? An invisible barrier that prevented them from going on.

However, it wasn't long before three magnificent fairies arrived to greet them all. They could see other fairies flying around in the near distance; it was a wonderful sight to behold. They were dressed immaculately in fine embroidered cottons, silks and colourful garments, with patterned skirts to match.

It was a breathtaking experience as the leader of the fairy group introduced herself and her escorts to the Chadwick family group. "Hello, friends of the earth. My name is Dianna, and this is Caroline, and this is Augusta. We have come to greet you all as our honoured guests. Please come and enter the wonderful world of Annatasia."

"But we can't go any further, because every time we try we get an electric shock," answered Billy Chadwick apprehensively.

"Oh, that is all right, we have turned off the power to the universal crystal detector. Nothing can harm you now. You are free to travel onwards to our wonderful world – a vista of paradise. The shock that you felt was an invisible electric field, which is there to stop any intruders from penetrating our perimeter fences, and which tells us that visitors have arrived. Unfortunately we have to have proper security procedures. And I have telepathically instructed headquarters that you are all friendly human beings. So come, my special friends, and explore and learn whilst we travel to the heart of the city of Annatasia," continued the leader of the fairies.

With that, all the Chadwicks looked at one another in sheer amazement and followed on foot. Everything around them was beautifully crafted, from the structure of the buildings to the lakes and pools. The surrounding landscape was covered in gorgeous wild flowers, with many species which they did not know.

There was much activity as hundreds of fairies were seen flying around the beautiful kingdom, landing and taking off as they travelled about on their daily tasks and activities.

'This surely must be heaven on earth – a special place like no other,' thought the Chadwick family.

Eventually they came to the entrance to the magnificent colourful city. Beautiful fairies came and showed them to their rooms inside the palatial fortress, which had its own unique drawbridge.

They were lucky enough to witness the May Day celebrations where young fairy children took it in turns to run around the giant maypole. There were many more exciting activities taking place, amid much gaiety and laughter.

Tired and weary from their adventures, they soon fell fast asleep, knowing that they were safe at last in the land of plenty. How privileged they all were!

The following morning they all awoke to the beautiful sounds of music – music like no other – classical in style, and so wonderful to hear, with the sound of the harp and other stringed instruments playing.

After they had all washed, they were invited to sit in the large banqueting hall. Everything in sight was beautifully crafted, with ornate chandeliers, gold-inlaid mirrors, skilfully made furniture, crystal glass windows and drawings and paintings. Exquisite cutlery, glass, earthenware, pottery, gold and silverware, Greek and Roman statuettes, busts and other Greek classical designs filled the palace of Annatasia. It was awe-inspiring, all hand-made by the fairies of nature, who seemed so pleasant, happy and mirthful. The joys of spring and summer were in the air.

Eventually, after absorbing all that beauty, they were

invited to meet the Queen of Annatasia, who would be sitting down at the head of the large mahogany table.

With much pomp and ceremony the beautiful Queen Theodora III came and sat down, with her trumpeters heralding her arrival.

After a couple of minutes, Billy Chadwick stood up and bowed before Her Majesty and introduced all of his family one by one.

The Fairy Queen smiled and acknowledged his presence. "Welcome, welcome, dear friends of Blackbird Wood. I hear that you have travelled far and wide through difficult terrain, through dense forests, woods, mountains and valleys. It cannot have been easy for you, with much danger and adversity to contend with, such as villainous spirits who have tried to prevent you from returning safely to your country cottage. There is not much that we do not know of your destiny and fate. You are safe here in my kingdom, and the treacherous misdeeds of Slobber Dom, Dom with his sidekick, Jingle Black Jack, and Silba the witch have not gone unnoticed. All the terrible things that they have done have been recorded in our unique records system. You are lucky to have survived these ordeals intact," said Theodora III authoritatively.

With that, Billy Chadwick bowed again, showing the monarch the respect she deserved. "Oh, great Queen of Annatasia, we are greatly humbled to be in your presence, and we are thankful for your hospitality. We cannot thank you enough. We have no money to repay you for all your services, only words to show our gratitude. We all pay great homage to you, Theodora III," said brave Billy with etiquette and manners.

"Why, thank you, young Billy Chadwick. It is nice of you to show me so much consideration. You are a true gentleman. There is no need to worry about money for repayment. You are all here at my pleasure, free of financial worries, because we live here at Annatasia free of human traditions where you are normally expected to pay for everything," said the charming, beautiful Queen.

"There is one thing that I truly wish for, Queen Theodora. Do you possess the powers to change someone back from a nasty spell that has been placed on them? In my group there are two who need your help urgently. Firstly, my brother, Peter, has been turned into a simple butterfly within the bottle that my sister, Alberta, carries with her, all because of Slobber Dom, Dom's tricks. And, secondly, Frederick the duck, as you can see, is now a sad wolf, due to the cleverness of Silba the witch of Blackbird Wood," said Billy Chadwick hopefully.

The Crown Princess and Queen Theodora III listened intently, then stood with her magic wand and asked Alberta to bring her glass jar and Frederick the wolf to her side. She released the butterfly from the jar and, with three waves of the wand, and the magical chant "Fairy, fairy, who is the fairest of them all, may this magic wand transfer you back to the fold," they were instantly changed back to their former selves.

Frederick the duck was so elated with extreme joy that he quacked, quacked and quacked for all the world to see. And with Peter back, the scene was one of much mirth and gaiety. With the evil spells now reversed, everyone became hopeful for the future again.

Billy bowed and bowed before Her Gracious Majesty, thanking her a million times over. Even Trojan the troll was immensely happy with this spectacular outcome. Both Peter and Frederick thanked the Fairy Queen for her unique assistance.

The Queen proclaimed, "Do not fear the invisible worlds, my friends. Slobber Dom, Dom and his cronies would never ever try to cause mischief within the territory of Annatasia. They are extremely scared of coming here, because they would be brought before the courts and punished for their crimes against humanity. We at court are well aware of their cunningness and

Bringing Back Produce from
the Enormous Gardens.

mischief, and have kept records of their wrongdoings. They are nothing but villains who reside in Blackbird Wood. Unfortunately they are undisciplined and reckless, and are envious of those who enjoy themselves immensely leading proper lives, and who only wish good fortune upon others, without the traits of jealously and greed."

The Chadwicks were then taken on a grand tour of Annatasia to see all the curiosities, buildings and other marvels it possessed, with Dianna, Caroline and Augusta as their escorts.

Outside were thousands and thousands of wonderful balloons, with their baskets full of fairies who travelled around the magnificent kingdom using the balloons to bring back produce (like marrows, turnips, carrots, potatoes, onions, cabbages and swedes, etc.) from the enormous gardens. All the fairies were self-sufficient, and grew all their own vegetables, working alongside nature, cultivating everything in a clean working environment.

They left Trojan behind because of his size and weight. He would be entertained by other fairies while they were away.

They all set off in two huge balloons. Other creatures were seen with haloes around their bodies. This intrigued the Chadwicks, because they had never seen such creatures before.

Elated by their experience, as the balloon went higher and higher into the atmosphere, they all tried to speak at once. Finally Peter asked, "Dianna, what are those beings who fly so fast through the air?"

"Oh, they are angels – angels of light, angels of mercy, angels of truth. They are all on different missions to rescue human beings from adversity, but only if their credit is good, though. They work alongside all the fairies, but at lightning speed. They are very special and they help people, and animals when they are in extreme danger. They are on a higher frequency than us, with beautiful auras containing the vibrant colours of the rainbow. Some are invisible and some, like those you see, work in the physical world, bringing hope to those mere mortals who do not understand the laws of nature. They answer certain prayers and wishes, and bring relief to human beings who are lost in the spiritual realms. We never interfere with them, because they are extremely busy guarding the young and old. They may have helped your family, without you knowing it, as you travelled alone in Blackbird Wood, by steering you away from trouble and mishap. Sometimes they allow humans to make their own mistakes, so they can learn through experience, for they cannot take away free will. But they do listen when you make a special wish that doesn't bring harm to anyone, especially when it concerns you praying for others who are in need of help. Unconditional love, my friends! If people prayed properly, then it would be a better world for humankind in the long term. Everyone has to learn and to appreciate life as we know it, with love and understanding. This is how everything in the fairy kingdom works out to our advantage: by being benevolent, thoughtful, showing consideration to others, showing respect, helping when asked, always being truthful and sincere, never taking from others what doesn't belong to you, being of service, and being charitable. These are the virtues of true happiness. We never expect anything in return, and also give unlimited love," said Dianna lovingly.

The balloons travelled to the east, where they slowly descended into a glorious park filled with a billion flowers, including roses, clematis, foxgloves, wild daisies, sunflowers, red poppies and ferns. Willow, oak, ash, elm, fir, silver birch and monkey puzzle trees also grew there along with many other species. All were being expertly cultivated with the loving care and attention of worker fairies, who seemed extremely happy working in this beautiful paradise.

They were then shown how to make their own soft

drinks. Worker bees, wasps and hummingbirds all ferried nectar to and fro in a never-ending cycle to manufacture soft drinks using the juices of apple, orange, plum, gooseberry, strawberry, pear, carrot and tomato. All the fairies helped out by squashing down the fermented fruits, which were stored for safe keeping until required. This was surely paradise on earth. The Chadwicks marvelled at each thing that was shown to them. Everyone was friendly and helpful in a unique world of pleasure and gaiety. The boys and girls were ecstatic, as were their grandparents.

After journeying back to the crystal palace of Annatasia, Arthur and Bella Chadwick were healed of their arthritis by two special fairies. They had both suffered from it for years, but a concoction of special herbs enabled them to walk without using a walking stick. They also began to look more youthful after they were taught how to exercise and eat properly. They were told to eat plenty of vegetables and fruit, like grapes, garlic, lemon and figs. Honey and cider were recommended but they were advised not to eat too much barley and wheat. Arthur and Bella Chadwick were over the moon at being healed from their arthritis, and gave many thanks to all the fairies involved.

On the third day at Annatasia, the Chadwicks were taken on a journey to visit all the different species of wildlife. They saw elephants, rhinoceroses, zebras, lions, tigers, bears, camels, monkeys and giraffes; ostriches, penguins, parrots and other birds; and several reptile species. They were all in their natural habitat, with invisible electromagnetic fields to stop the creatures from wandering from their enclosures. It was so unique and magical that all the animals could speak to one another. Even the lions and tigers were friendly, not like wild ones in Africa or Asia.

They were then shown a beautiful winged white horse, named Renaldo, who could fly unaided through the heavens above the earth, free as a bird in flight.

Billy was asked if he wanted to fly with Dianna on Renaldo for the journey of a lifetime. The offer was too good not to be taken up, so off he went, sitting behind Dianna. The horse took off and its beautiful white wings flapped gracefully through the air. They flew above the kingdom and could see below all the wonderful fields being cultivated by the thousands of fairies going about their business. Renaldo flew for ten miles, then returned several times to pick up a different passenger, until they had all had a ride, except for Trojan who was too heavy. What great fun they had riding on the magical horse, free as the wind, free of time and space! Even Frederick the duck had a go, and was frightened a little, so Alberta held him close to her body. Poor old Trojan had to wait and wait for them to finish, but all the fairies kept him in good spirits by telling him plenty of fairy stories.

Following that experience they were taken to a large indoor pool where they could bathe and relax. Trojan used his large wooden club, waving it from side to side to make large waves in the warm water as the Chadwicks learned how to swim correctly. All the fairies chuckled merrily at the spectacle of Trojan climbing carefully down into the spring waters and swimming like a fish. The classical backdrop of colonnades, the portico entrance, Greek busts and sculptures on white marble columns, classical pictures and exotic plants gave one the feel of being in ancient Rome or Greece.

Chapter Seven

Silba Casts More Spells

After their evening meal at the palace, they all retired to their individual rooms, with four-poster beds and silk and cotton mosquito nets, which were strung across to give one a peaceful rest, free from any disturbance.

But all was not well, because Silba the witch and her two accomplices were active and engaged in making spells of one kind or another.

With toads, newts and earwigs she ranted, while Slobber Dom, Dom and Jingle Black Jack looked on, both mesmerised by her chanting and hysterical outbursts. Zuppy, her magical cat, and Saladin, the naughty baboon, came into the grotto in a trance-like state, induced by Silba and her magical rites.

"Oh, cackle, cackle, cackle. Please bring the north winds to bear, and bring down the kingdom of Annatasia. Oh, Theodora! Oh, Theodora of crystal heaven, you have crossed me not once, not twice but threefold. May thunder and rain come to spoil, and strike your realm to ruins. I now throw this salt before the moon. May all the stars disappear, and bring lightning strikes so severe to flood your mighty kingdom bare."

"Oh, what have you done, Silba? Won't we all get into trouble?" questioned Slobber Dom, Dom quietly.

"Oh, you stupid sprite, it is our magical right to make these spells work. One fine day everything will be mine, all mine, for Theodora III has reigned for too long already, and those Chadwicks will all disappear as if they have never existed. Who do they think they are? They come to my grotto expecting to get rich quick with rich-quick schemes where I do all the work. I shall be the new ruler of an empire never seen before," raged Silba with her spiteful attitude.

"Oh, Silba, thou art the cleverest witch around, for I would never have guessed in a million years what your real intentions were," replied Slobber Dom, Dom slyly.

"That's because I have the brains and you do not. I have planned this for years and years. And tonight they shall all feel my anger," cackled the witch whilst rocking and rocking with her many meditations.

Jingle Black Jack looked on whilst licking his black paws and smiling to himself. The cunning cat was thinking how he could turn this to his own advantage. He was happy to let Slobber Dom, Dom get the earbashing from Silba, who had no time for slackers and time-wasters.

"Tonight, tonight I shall order the forces of nature to bring complete havoc upon the land of Annatasia, and turn Theodora's fine kingdom to ashes. She will burn brightly before the waxing moon fades," exploded Silba in a frightening stance as she placed more and more insects into her large black cauldron. She stirred in mice, rats and insects, huffing and puffing loudly whilst visualising herself as the new ruler of Annatasia.

She gave everyone a pouch of magical ingredients to scatter at the midnight hour and told them they were to carry out her instructions to the letter.

At the appointed time of 11.30 p.m., with Silba, Saladin and Zuppy on her magical broom, accompanied by Slobber Dom, Dom and Jingle Black Jack, they all set off flying through the darkened skies and grey clouds to create as much mayhem as possible.

At the appointed time, they flew three times in an anticlockwise direction before dropping their herbs and spells over the sleeping inhabitants of Annatasia city.

A few minutes after twelve, Peter awoke sweating profusely from a nightmare in which he vividly saw Silba the witch flying upon her magical broom. After drinking mouthful after mouthful of water, he came from his bed and went intuitively to the palace window, where he looked up at the night-time sky, where a million stars shone down. 'So peaceful,' he thought, 'so very peaceful indeed.' He looked again and saw Silba the witch fly past in the shadow of the copper moon. What trick was this before his eyes?

The night air became freezing, the wind whipped up in a great burst of anger like a hurricane, the night became stormy in a wild frenzy and large, dangerous hailstones began hitting the palace a million times over. What curse was this? Where moments before it had been a beautiful evening with the stars of heaven sparkling brightly, now the tempest wind was circulating throughout the large palace of Annatasia.

With everyone now awake, a thousand fairies mustered in the great hall where Queen Theodora III held her council as the fierce winds gained momentum. There was an eerie ghostly feel as they were sent outside to check that everything that was movable was secured and tied down satisfactorily. The unusual wind was hard and unabating. Strong gusts were blowing at nearly 100 miles per hour and heavy bursts of rain brought an unstoppable deluge of water.

The Chadwicks rose from their beds, dressed themselves, and went to the great hall for instructions. Queen Theodora III was sitting in her high chair of office, giving directions to her loyal army of worker fairies.

"I, Theodora III, am holding court during this destructive hour. A severe battle has been started by none other than Silba the witch from the dark recesses of the underworld. She has used black magic with her many rituals. We are being attacked as I speak. The weather she has changed to her own advantage, and a

"The Battle for Liberty Has Begun."

storm is prevalent over Annatasia during this midnight hour. I have confirmation of her involvement, with her other confederates and comrades, from our night patrols. Her cronies seem quite happy to carry out all of her secret desires. She will stop at nothing to prevent us from living our lives in peace and harmony with our neighbours. As you can imagine, Slobber Dom, Dom and Jingle Black Jack are involved. They come this dark hour to take my kingdom from me, so they can rule through fear and intimidation, but this beautiful land is not theirs for the taking. I, Theodora III, am the rightful ruler. As you know, I govern fairly and squarely. This is a time for action. Normally we are peace-abiding citizens, and liberty rules within all my lands, but we cannot be complacent; the time has come to fight for our idyllic way of life."

As Her Majesty spoke three towers collapsed from the onslaught of the wild weather, bringing devastation amongst her people. But how was she to stop the perpetrators of mischief?

Trojan presented himself before the Queen and bowed. He asked if he could be of assistance during this terrible hour.

"Oh, brave Trojan, any help will be a godsend, but what can you do?" questioned Theodora III daringly.

"Billy Chadwick and myself are willing to go back and destroy the witch's grotto. With my heavy club I can do much damage to her wicked, devious plans. I, Trojan, shall save your home and lands from any further mischief that is afoot."

"Very well then. You may leave my lands and infiltrate our mortal enemy's defences. Normally I would not seek to destroy any person, animal or insect, but this is different. We must bring all who do not hold any morals whatsoever to justice. The battle for liberty has begun in earnest, so go forth, mighty one, and save the kingdom from these mercenaries of destruction."

Trojan and Billy escaped undetected through the

gales. They had to journey some thirty miles into the interior of the forest.

Young Billy hid inside Trojan's leather pouch so the titan's giant strides could cover the ground quickly. Trojan demolished all the vegetation before him, and the earth shook under the deafening thud, thud, thud of his feet.

After two hours of hard walking through bush, field and valley they arrived at the witch's grotto. They immediately set to work, quickly smashing everything in sight. All her talismans, trinkets, medals, hieroglyphs, good-luck charms and other magical aids were ruined. Her large black cauldron was overturned, spilling out all of the dead creatures and insects which were used in her magic spells.

Both Trojan and Billy then hid themselves in the green undergrowth to patiently wait for the witch to return.

After three long hours the witch approached, along with Slobber Dom, Dom and Jingle Black Jack. All were screaming with delight at the havoc they had caused.

"Oh, Jingle Black Jack, we have succeeded tenfold. My spells have worked their vengeance on the fairy kingdom of Annatasia. The mighty palace is destroyed, and I am the new ruler. Oh, come inside the grotto and have a celebratory drink and make a toast for old times' sake. Oh, come in, my two best friends, and give thanks to the earthly moon," cackled the evil witch proudly.

In all of the excitement it wasn't until Silba had landed safely in amongst the green ferns that, to her horror, she could see the devastation all about her. She screamed and screamed out aloud at the destruction.

Saladin and Zuppy went mad as they climbed amongst the ruins, whilst showing their mistress all the broken objects which were destroyed beyond recognition.

With her grotto in complete ruins, Silba's emotions exploded. "Where art thou, those that creep and hide amongst the woods and forest. Come and show yourselves this dark hour, for I smell sweat and fear underneath the bright copper moon," tempted Silba slyly.

Young Billy whispered to Trojan, "What goes around comes around. You deserve everything you get. You cannot go around simply destroying everything in your path, Silba."

The witch was enraged as she searched frantically for anything that may have survived, but nothing was retrievable, and she looked up at the moon, cursing and cursing at her misfortunes. Her base had been completely ruined beyond recognition by the hand of unseen beings.

Smiling with victory, Trojan and Billy Chadwick made their way back to Annatasia with complete joy in their hearts. Silba had been taught a hard lesson – not to mess about with magic and the like.

On their return, they immediately went to the great hall of Annatasia and gave a good account of their destruction of the grotto.

The Queen was ecstatic and, now that the terrible winds had finally abated, everything that had been destroyed within the palace could be rebuilt, better than before. Fairies were instructed to redesign the ruined palace.

Both Trojan and Billy were awarded Annatasia's highest medal for extreme bravery for their lone mission through the forest of Blackbird Wood.

When the morning light appeared repairing the devastation was paramount to those brave citizens of Annatasia. Hundreds of balloon baskets had been turned over and smashed, the flower and vegetable gardens were wrecked beyond recognition and there was much structural damage as well.

Meanwhile, Theodora III ordered her elite troops of fairies to go into the forest and capture Silba and her cohorts so they could be brought to justice.

Heavily Damaged by Trojan's
Wooden Club.

For three whole days and nights they searched and searched, starting at her grotto, but nowhere could she be found. No clues to her whereabouts could be found in her grotto, which had been heavily damaged by Trojan's large wooden club. But it was imperative that she be found sooner rather than later to face criminal charges of mass destruction.

Day after day the fairies were sent out combing the whole area for news of their disappearance. Even Renaldo, the white winged horse, was brought in to help in their frantic searches. Instructions were given to be as careful as possible when the time came to apprehend them. It was known that they could use magical practices to become invisible, and that they had the power to change themselves into other beings with their clever magical spells.

Even though the witch had extreme powers and knowledge at her beck and call, it was thought that given enough time and enough rope they would hang themselves, because they could not stop causing trouble amongst the good citizens of Blackbird Wood and the many districts of Anatasia. But it was unthinkable to allow them any freedom. The fairies' report book and diary was filled with incidents of all the horrendous crimes committed in their insatiable quest for power. The corruptible power of persuasion and destruction, with magic as its foundation, had been brought into operation by its user, the witch, Silba. No one was safe while she and her comrades were left to do their evil work in a cunning and devious way. Annatasia could have been completely destroyed by Silba's spells and potions in an act of war against the fairy kingdom.

It was whilst at dinner in the great hall that the Chadwicks discussed what had taken place.

"Are they completely stupid with their cunning cat-and-mouse games?" asked Samantha studiously.

"I'm afraid they are – no commonsense at all amongst them," replied Dianna, the head fairy, wisely.

"Oh, they can't have any brains between them all," said Alberta excitedly.

"Brains? A child of two has got more sense than them all put together. There is no logic at all. It is purely greed and envy that spurs them on with their wicked plans, which seem to backfire most times," replied Dianna.

"That can only mean one thing. The dark side of their personalities is attracted to magical rites, but that magic can only work for a short time. It is a dangerous practice that brings to its operator a lesson not to dabble with things he does not understand," advised Augusta willingly.

"So, children from Buttercup Cottage, always remember, never ever dabble with the occult, as it is called. Leave it to idiots and clever Dicks, for its glamour is nothing more than an illusion imprinted upon the mind. They are not prepared to work for a living, so they turn to magic in its purest form to attain things which are not rightly theirs in the first place. They are unwittingly robbing from the universe, where Nature, supreme with all her wisdom, teaches man that appreciation and kindness is really a strength, not a weakness," advised Caroline wisely.

Chapter Eight

A Trap Is Set

All of the fairies were occupied with their daily patrols, important tasks and schedules. The Chadwicks helped clear up all the wreckage that had been caused by imbeciles who knew no better and had put lives at risk through their jealousy, envy and greed.

Trojan, because of his immense size, picked up all the large stones and crystals that had fallen down during the onslaught of the horrendous winds. He cleared a suitable path around the most damaged areas of the palace, and picked up all the balloons that had been wrecked.

New plans were drawn up by the fairies to rebuild the damaged palace of Annatasia in a better format than before. Their engineers presented the new designs to Queen Theodora III before the work was allowed to start.

It wasn't long before everyone was employed bringing large amounts of crystal from the stone quarries to finally start construction. They were as busy as bumblebees in their hives.

Special fairies started clearing all the damaged flowers and vegetable gardens, to replant in a show of strength and commitment.

No, Silba would not win this battle with her devious cunning tricks. Had she and her group of wayward malefactors gone underground away from detection, shying away from trouble for the time being? Rumours of her possible hiding place were numerous, with so many making suggestions as to where she might be.

Everything was becoming shipshape once more as worked progressed. A team of workers went around singing quietly to themselves as the giant palace took shape once more.

Extra fairies were put on full alert for any more incoming attacks – better to be prepared than not! Every precaution was put into place to stop the madness from happening again. Annatasia was to be made as impenetrable as any fortress could be. All the fairies were engaged in placing more electromagnetic fields around the boundaries of Annatasia to prevent any breaches in its defence.

After two months of hard labour, the kingdom of Annatasia had been rebuilt with loving care and attention. No detail had been overlooked.

Although there was no news of Silba's whereabouts, the Chadwicks decided it was time for them to move on and find their way back to Buttercup Cottage. After many goodbyes, the Chadwicks thanked Theodora III for her unique hospitality and help. They were to follow a route mapped out by the head fairy, Dianna. It would be forty miles as the crow flies to their final destination.

All the fairies not on duty came to see the Chadwicks leave. They were given food hampers and water, and told not to trust any strangers that they might meet on their long journey home – although who would attack them with Trojan at their side? They would have to be mad as a mad hatter to try their luck.

So off they went, after their farewells, into the interior of the forest, singing gaily whilst chopping down the green undergrowth as they proceeded.

After five miles they again met Sniggy Bells, who

seemed to materialise out of thin air. The happy, carefree leprechaun was seen chatting to himself with words they did not understand in their entirety.

"Hocus pocus, babble de babble. Oh, the luck of the Irish quick," or words to that effect.

"Fancy seeing you again!" said Alberta excitedly.

All the Chadwicks stopped to take a breather and gathered around the cheeky leprechaun to hear what news he might have.

"Oh, me favourite chums of the forest, are ye lost again, unable to find your way out?" asked the leprechaun whilst smoking his long black pipe.

"Oh, no, we do know this time where we are, because the head fairy of Annatasia has given us a precise map so we can proceed on our long, hazardous journey," said Bella Chadwick wisely.

"Oh, that is good, then. Top of the morning to ye all. And I see Trojan is with ye once more – not a beast to mix with, I should say," replied the leprechaun happily.

"You are right with your assumption, Sniggy Bells," said Samantha lightly.

"Do you, Mr Leprechaun, have any information about Silba, Slobber Dom, Dom and his wicked sidekick, Jingle Black Jack?" asked Peter hesitantly.

"Oh, me chums, ye have certainly hit upon a raw nerve to ask me of those foolish beings. They are very much alive and active – licking their wounds, as one might say. It was only yesterday that I spied upon them. They are holed up in a cave complex, some twenty-five miles from here, on the edge of the forest, eastwards from this point – up to no good, I can report."

"Why haven't you reported your find to the fairies of Annatasia?" questioned Billy quickly.

"Because, because I don't like to interfere with things that are nothing to do with me. If Silba, the old hag, knew that I was the one that squealed, then I would be changed into an animal – or worse, an insect that creeps around – to roam the world on me own,"

Renaldo, the White Winged Horse.

replied the wise leprechaun.

With that, Trojan placed his large wooden club underneath Sniggy Bell's chin and warned him of the consequences if he were lying. "Very well, then, Mr Leprechaun, we shall let you off this time. I do hope for your sake that you are telling us the truth," said the weary troll.

"Oh, but I am. I would not lie to ye on such a delicate matter as I have just described. I would not lead ye into a trap with a devious plan," replied the leprechaun hesitantly. With that, Sniggy Bells disappeared from sight – to where, was anybody's guess.

On they all travelled until late the next day, when they finally arrived at Buttercup Cottage. All the vines and thorns were still visible, wrapped tightly around the white cottage.

Trojan immediately started to wrench the wild plants free, making short work of the thorns, uprooting them and collecting them for burning, to allow the Chadwicks entry into their home.

The next day Dianna and Caroline arrived, flying on the back of Renaldo, the white winged horse, to check upon their friends' safe arrival in Blackbird Wood. They also brought the Chadwicks gifts, including eight rose quartz crystals, which acted as transmitters and receivers. If the Chadwicks got into trouble, then they could immediately use the crystals to contact the fairy patrols by telepathic thoughts, which would vibrate out a distress signal.

The Chadwicks informed the head fairy, Dianna, of the witch's whereabouts. She was pleased to learn of this and promised that on their return to Annatasia they would devise a plan to capture the witch and her friends.

The fairies stayed for the day, then waved goodbye to their friends.

The Chadwicks settled back into a routine of domestic happiness, and they were all employed in building a large log cabin for Trojan's use. Even Frederick the duck, from Nottingham, was pleased as Punch to be living with the Chadwicks, especially Joe and Alberta, who had befriended him and fed him, and now protected him from harm and malice.

Three days passed, then an old hag arrived at Buttercup Cottage. She said she was a travelling Romany who was selling bric-a-brac, herbs, lotions and potions and who was in need of rest.

"Oh, cackle, cackle. Do you want to buy these lotions and potions to make you healthy and prosperous? Come and see for yourself what I, Griselda, have in my large wicker basket. Yes, I can say with authority that these medicines can make you lucky beyond your wildest dreams. Oh, come, all you children, and taste my new medicines," chanted the old wrinkly hag.

The Chadwicks all lined up to see what remedies were on offer; then they gave her food and water.

But all was not well, because the travelling hag was none other than Silba the witch in disguise. She saw the Chadwicks as mortal enemies. They had wrecked all of her careful plans and she wanted revenge.

They invited her to join them at their dinner table, so Griselda went indoors and sat down with a cunning smile. "Oh, you won't regret this favour. You are so kind and helpful – especially to an old woman who has travelled far and wide."

"Oh, that is all right, Griselda. We are grateful that you have come amongst us. It's not every day we get to see a stranger around these parts of Blackbird Wood," said Arthur Chadwick invitingly.

"Everything is fine, old lady of the woods. What is ours is yours, Griselda," said Bella Chadwick.

As it was mealtime, Griselda persuaded the Chadwicks to add to their food the special herbs that she had brought with her, which Bella Chadwick did trustingly. But this was a trick, because unbeknown to the Chadwicks the witch had mixed in with her other herbs two poisonous plants – deadly nightshade and hemlock – which can send you into a deep, deep sleep that you never ever recover from.

They ate the meal and, after some ten minutes, all the Chadwicks fell asleep. Then the witch flew away on her broomstick.

But the witch had forgotten about Trojan, who was away deep in the woods with his axe, chopping up tree trunks for his log cabin. On his return all was quiet, with just the sound of the birds in the trees close by; but, whilst dropping his load of wood, intuitively Trojan detected something was wrong. There were no children playing outside, which was most unusual. He went to the cottage and peered frantically through the windows. Through the kitchen window he could see that all the Chadwicks were asleep and there was no movement or sound coming from within the eerie cottage.

Trojan quickly fetched one of the crystals the fairies had given them. He screamed out, maddened by his find, and prayed with all his heart and mind, mentally sending out his thoughts for assistance.

It wasn't long before a fairy patrol, with fairy wings, like beautiful butterflies dancing the dragonfly dance, arrived. Around and around the cottage the fairies flew in all of directions. Then three head fairies, like orbs of light, went down the chimney pot.

When they reached the sleeping occupants, one fairy waved her magic wand and said, "Awake, awake from your laboured sleep, and reverse this magic while we sweep." With confidence the fairy repeated her chant three times in succession.

Soon there were signs of life, and happily the Chadwicks all awoke from their deep spellbound sleep.

All the fairies smiled. They told the Chadwicks that they would apprehend Silba quickly before she could do any more damage. In the middle of the forest all the fairies hid themselves amongst the trees and other vegetation and baited a trap. Silba, Slobber Dom, Dom

Safe Again.

and Jingle Black Jack fell straight into their clever ambush, and they were arrested and taken to Annatasia to stand trial for their crimes.

At last Blackbird Wood was safe again, with no bad sprites or witches making life hell for the good citizens of the forest. And the Chadwicks lived amongst the good fairies happily ever after.

What happened to Silba and her comrades? You may well ask, dear reader. They were given ten years in jail for their bad behaviour, and were eventually taught how to become good citizens and show respect to others, without the use of magical aids and the like.